"We have to talk."

"No, we really don't." Isabelle wasn't going to give an inch. She wasn't even sure why Wes was there, and if he didn't know the whole truth, then she wasn't going to give him any information. The only important thing was getting rid of him before he could see Caroline.

"That's not gonna fly," he said and moved in, putting both hands on her shoulders to ease her out of the way.

The move caught her so off guard, Isabelle didn't even try to hold her ground. He was already walking into the house before she could stop him. And even as she opened her mouth to protest, his arm brushed against her and she shivered. It wasn't fear stirring inside her, not even trepidation. It was desire.

The same flush of need that had happened to her years ago whenever Wes was near. Almost from the first minute she'd met him, that jolt of something more had erupted between them. She'd never felt anything like it before Wes—or since.

"I think I deserve an explanation," he said tightly.

"You *deserve*?" she repeated, in little more than a hiss. She shot a quick look down the hall toward the kitchen where Caroline was.

"You should have told me about our daughter."

* * *

The Tycoon's Secret Child is part of the series Texas Cattleman's Club: Blackmail—No secret—or heart—is safe in Royal, Texas...

Dear Reader,

Being a part of the Texas Cattleman's Club continuity is always fun for a writer. Not only do we get to revisit Royal, Texas—but we get the opportunity to work with a lot of very talented writers and our wonderful editors.

In this book, *The Tycoon's Secret Child*, you'll meet Wes Jackson, a man who started his first fledgling business in college. Now that business is in danger because someone is blackmailing him. The scandal threatens an important merger—but for Wes, the important part is that he's just discovered he's a father!

Isabelle Graystone was in love with Wes but left him five years ago when she knew he would never love her in return. She took with her the secret of her pregnancy.

When Wes finds out about their daughter, Caroline, nothing is going to keep him away. He and Isabelle will have to work together toward a compromise they can all live with. Sounds easy—but it won't be.

I really hope you enjoy this trip back to Royal as much as I did!

Happy reading!

Maureen Child

MAUREEN CHILD

THE TYCOON'S SECRET CHILD

Special thanks and acknowledgment are given to Maureen Child for her contribution to the Texas Cattleman's Club: Blackmail miniseries.

Recycling programs for this product may not exist in your area.

ISBN-13: 978-0-373-83818-9

The Tycoon's Secret Child

This edition published by arrangement with Harlequin Books S.A.

For questions and comments about the quality of this book, please contact us at CustomerService@Harlequin.com.

Printed in U.S.A.

Maureen Child writes for the Harlequin Desire line and can't imagine a better job. A seven-time finalist for a prestigious Romance Writers of America RITA® Award, Maureen is an author of more than one hundred romance novels. Her books regularly appear on bestseller lists and have won several awards, including a Prism Award, a National Readers' Choice Award, a Colorado Romance Writers Award of Excellence and a Golden Quill Award. She is a native Californian but has recently moved to the mountains of Utah.

Books by Maureen Child

Harlequin Desire

The Fiancée Caper
After Hours with Her Ex
Triple the Fun
Double the Trouble
The Baby Inheritance
Maid Under the Mistletoe

Pregnant by the Boss

Having Her Boss's Baby
A Baby for the Boss
Snowbound with the Boss

Texas Cattleman's Club: Blackmail

The Tycoon's Secret Child

Visit her Author Profile page at Harlequin.com, or maureenchild.com, for more titles.

To the world's greatest editors,
Stacy Boyd and Charles Griemsman—
in the world of writers and editors,
you two shine. Writing isn't always easy
but you guys bring out the best in all of us.

One

Wesley Jackson sat in his corporate office in Houston, riding herd on the department heads attending the meeting he'd called. It had been a long two hours, and he was about done. Thankfully, things were winding down now and he could get out of the city. He didn't mind coming into town once in a while, but he always seemed to breathe deeper and easier back home in Royal.

Didn't appear to matter how successful he became, he'd always be a small-town guy at the heart of it. Just as, he thought with an inner smile as he set one booted foot on his knee, you couldn't take Texas out of the businessman.

"Am I keeping you from something important?" Wes asked suddenly when he noticed Mike Stein, the youngest man on his PR team, staring out a window from the other side of his wide mahogany desk.

Mike flinched. He was energetic, usually eager, but a little distracted today. Not hard to understand, Wes thought, considering it was January 2 and everyone in the office was probably nursing the dregs of a hangover from various New Year's parties. And Wes could cut the kid a small break, but that was done now.

"What?" Mike blurted. "No, absolutely not. Sorry."

Tony Danvers snorted, then hid the sound behind a cough.

Wes's gaze slid to him, then to the woman sitting on the other side of him. Mike was new, but talented and driven. Tony knew his way around the company blindfolded, and Donna Higgs had her finger on the pulse of every department in the building. The three of them exemplified exactly what he expected from his employees. Dedication. Determination. Results.

Since everything else he'd wanted discussed had been covered in the last two hours, Wes finally brought up the most important item on his agenda.

"The Just Like Me line," he said, flicking a glance at Tony Danvers. "Any problems? We on track for spring delivery to outlets?"

This new doll was destined to be the biggest thing in the country. At least, he told himself, that was the plan. There were dolls that could be specially ordered to look like a child, of course. But Wes's company had the jump on even them. With the accessories available and the quick turnaround, the Just Like Me doll was going to smash all sales record previously set for...*anything.* He smiled to himself just thinking about it. A line of dolls that looked like their owners. Parents could find a doll that resembled their child, either online or at retail locations. Or they could special order one with accessories to make it even more like the child in question.

Wes once considered bringing the doll out early, to catch the Christmas shopping frenzy. But he'd decided against it, banking on the fact that by February children would already be tired of their Christmas toys and looking for something new.

He was counting on making such an impact that by *next* Christmas, the dolls would be on every kid's wish list. And every child who had already received one would be looking for another. Maybe one in the image of a best friend or a sibling.

The possibilities were endless.

Tony sat back in his brown leather chair, hooked one ankle on a knee. "We're right on schedule, boss. We've got dozens of different designs of dolls. Every ethnicity, every hair type I've ever heard of, and a few that were news to me."

"You're so male," Donna Higgs, the marketing director, muttered with a shake of her head.

Tony winked at her. "Thanks for noticing."

Wes grinned but not at the two friends' byplay. His company, Texas Toy Goods Inc., was going to be the most talked-about toy company in the country once these dolls hit. Marketing, under Donna's steady hand, was already set for a huge campaign, he had the PR department set to flood social media, and a test group of kids had already proclaimed the doll a winner. After ten years of steady growth, Wes's company was poised for a jump that would change Wes from a multimillionaire to a billionaire practically overnight.

He'd started his company on not much more than a shoestring. He had had ideas, a partner he'd managed to buy out several years ago and a small inheritance from his father. With that, and his own driving ambition, Wes built a reputation for coming up with new ways of doing things in a centuries-old industry. He was known for his innovation and creativity. Thanks to him, and the best employees in the business, they'd built on their early successes until TTG was a presence in the toy industry. And the Just Like Me doll was going to give them that one last push over the top.

Each doll was unique in its own way and was going to appeal to every child on the planet. He had visions of European distribution as well, and knew that soon Texas Toy Goods was going to be an unstoppable force in the industry. And that wasn't even counting the upcoming merger he was working on with Teddy Bradford, the current CEO of PlayCo, or his other ventures under the Texas brand umbrella.

"So," Wes said, bringing them back on topic, "if the parent doesn't find exactly what they're looking for, we're set up for them to order specifics."

"Absolutely." Tony straightened up then leaned forward, bracing his forearms on his knees. "There'll be a kiosk in every toy department. The computer will link them to us and they can put in an order for any specific detail they need. Say, if the child has a prosthetic, we can match it. If the child has a specific disability, we're prepared for everything. From wheelchairs to braces, we can give every child out there the feeling of being special. Having a doll in their own image. Naturally, specific orders would take a little longer..."

Wes frowned. "How much longer?"

"Negligible," Donna put in. She checked something on her iPad and looked up at him. "I know Tony's production, but in marketing, we've been working with turnaround time so we can advertise it. With the wide array of dolls already available, we can put out a special order in a couple of days."

"That works." Nodding now, Wes leaned back in his own chair. "Make sure the factory floor is up to speed on this, and I want a centralized area devoted *only* to this project."

"Uh, boss?" Mike Stein held up one hand as if he were in class. But then, he was young and enthusiastic and would eventually get used to the more wide-open discussions Wes preferred during meetings.

"What is it?"

Mike glanced at the others before looking back at Wes. "We've got the ads lined up and the social media blast is ready to roll on the day."

"Good."

"But," Mike added, "I know it's not my department—"

"Doesn't matter," Wes told him. He liked his people being interested in *all* departments, not just their specialties.

"Okay. I was thinking, having a dedicated area at the factory could be problematic."

Tony actually leaned a little toward the left, putting some distance between himself and the new guy. At least the others knew better than to tell Wes something couldn't be done.

"Why's that?" Wes asked calmly.

"Well, it means pulling people off the line and setting them up to handle *only* these special orders."

"And?"

"Well," Mike continued, clearly unwilling to back off the track he found himself on. Wes could give him points for having guts. "That means we have people who are standing there *waiting* for something to do instead of working on the line and getting actual work done."

"What changes would you suggest?" Wes asked coolly.

Tony cleared his throat and gave a barely there shake of his head, trying to tell the kid in code to just shut up and let this one go. But Mike had the bit in his teeth now and wouldn't drop it.

"I would leave them working on the line and pull them out when a special order came in and then—"

"I appreciate your idea," Wes said, tapping his fingers against the gray leather blotter on his desk. "I want my people to feel free to speak up. But you're new here, Mike, and you need to learn that at TTG, we do things a little differently. Here, the customer is always number one. We design toys and the delivery system to facilitate the people who buy our toys. So if that means we have a separate crew waiting for the special orders to come in, then that's what we do. We're the best. That's what breeds success."

"Right." Mike nodded, swallowed hard and nodded again. "Absolutely. Sorry."

"No problem." Wes waved the apology away. He'd either learn from this and pick up on the way things were done at TTG, or the kid would leave and find a job somewhere else.

But damn, when did he start thinking of guys in their twenties as *kids*? When did Wes get ancient? He squashed that thought immediately. Hell, at thirty-four, he wasn't old. He was just *busy.* Running his company ate up every moment of every damn day. He was so busy, his social life was a joke. He couldn't even remember the last time he'd been with a woman. But that would come. Eventually. Right now, TTG demanded and deserved his full concentration.

Of course, his brain whispered, it hadn't always been that way. There'd been one woman—

Wes cut all thoughts of her off at the pass. That was done. Over. He hadn't been interested in long-term and she'd all but had *marriage and children* tattooed across her forehead. He'd had to end it and he wasn't sorry. Most of the time.

Having a relationship with one of his employees hadn't been a particularly smart move on his part. And sure, there'd been gossip and even resentment from some of his staff. But Wes hadn't been able to resist Belle. What the two of them had shared was like nothing he'd ever known. For a time, Wes had been willing to put up with whispers at work for the pleasure of being with Belle.

But it was over. The past.

"We've got the accessories covered, I think," Donna said. "When the special orders come in, we'll be able to turn them around in a flash."

"Good to hear. And if you don't have it?" Wes asked.

"We'll get it." Donna nodded sharply. "No problem on this, boss. It's going to work as smoothly as you expect it to. And it's going to be the biggest doll to hit the market since the vegetable patch babies back in the '80s."

"That's what I want to hear." Wes stood up, shoved both hands into his pockets and said, "That's all for now. Keep me in the loop."

Tony laughed. "Boss, everybody runs everything by you."

One corner of Wes's mouth quirked. "Yeah. Just the way I like it. Okay, back to work."

He watched them go, then told his assistant, Robin, to get him some fresh coffee. He'd need it once he started going through business emails. Inevitably, there were problems to walk through with suppliers, manufacturers, bankers and everyone else who either had a piece—or wanted one—of the Texas Toy Goods pie. But instead of taking a seat behind his desk, he walked across the wide office to the corner windows. The view of Houston was familiar, impressive. High-rises, glass walls reflecting sunlight that could blind a man. Thick white clouds sailing across a sky so blue it hurt the eyes.

He liked the city fine, but it wasn't somewhere he wanted to spend too much time. At least twice a week, he made the drive in from Royal, Texas, and his home office, to oversee accounts personally and on-site. He believed in having his employees used to seeing him there. People tended to get complacent when there was an absentee boss in the picture. But if he had a choice, he'd pick Royal over Houston.

His hometown had less traffic, less noise and the best burgers in Texas at the Royal Diner. Not to mention the fact that the memories in Royal were easier to live with than the ones centered here, in his office. Just being here, he remembered late-night work sessions with the woman he refused to think about. All-night sessions that had become a blistering-hot affair that had crashed and burned the minute she whispered those three deadly words—*I love you.* Even after all this time, that moment infuriated him. And despite—maybe *because* of—how it ended, that one woman stayed in his mind, always at the edges of his thoughts.

"What is it with women?" he asked the empty room. "Everything was going fine and then she just had to ruin it."

Of course, a boss/employee relationship wasn't going to work for the long haul anyway, and he'd known that going in. And even with the way things had ended, he couldn't completely regret any of it. What bothered him was that even now, five years later, thoughts of Belle kept cropping up as if his mind just couldn't let go.

A brisk knock on the door had him shaking his head and pushing thoughts of her to the back of his mind, where, hopefully, they would stay. "Come in."

Robin entered, carrying a tray with a single cup, a thermal carafe of coffee and a plate of cookies. He smiled. "What would I do without you?"

"Starve to death, probably," she said. Robin was in her forties, happily married and the proud mother of four. She loved her job, was damn good at it and kept him apprised of everything going on down here when he was in Royal. If she ever threatened to quit, Wes was prepared to offer her whatever she needed to stay.

"You scared the kid today."

Snorting a laugh as he remembered the look of sheer panic on Mike's face, Wes sat down at his desk and poured the first of what would be several cups of coffee. "He'll survive."

"Yeah, he will. A little fear's good. Builds character."

One eyebrow lifted as Wes laughed. "Your kids must be terrified of you."

"Me?" she asked. "Nope. I raise them tougher than that."

Wes chuckled.

"Harry called. He's headed into that meeting in New York. Said he'd call when he had it wrapped up."

Harry Baker, his vice president, was currently doing all the traveling around the country, arranging for the expedited shipping the new doll line would require. "That's good. Thanks."

After she left, Wes sipped at his coffee, took a cookie, had a bite, then scrolled to his email account. Idly, he scanned the forty latest messages, deleting the crap. He scanned the subject lines ruthlessly, until he spotted Your secret is out.

"What the hell?" Even while a part of his mind was thinking *virus or an ad for timeshares in Belize*, he clicked on the message and read it. Everything in him went cold and still. The cookie turned to ash in his mouth and he drank the coffee only to wash it down.

Look where your dallying has gotten you, the email read.

Check your Twitter account. Your new handle is Deadbeatdad. So you want to be the face of a new toy empire? Family friendly? Think again.

It was signed, Maverick.

"Who the hell is Maverick and what the hell is he talking about?" There was an attachment with the email, and even though Wes had a bad feeling about all of this, he opened it. The photograph popped onto his computer screen.

He shot to his feet, the legs of his chair scraping against the polished wooden floor like a screech. Staring down at the screen, his gaze locked on the image of the little girl staring back at him. "What the—"

She looked just like him. The child had Wes's eyes and a familiar smile and if that wasn't enough to convince him, which it was, he focused on the necklace the girl was wearing. Before he and Belle broke up, Wes had given her a red plastic heart on a chain of plastic beads. At the time, he'd used it as a joke gift right before giving her a pair of diamond earrings.

And the little girl in the photo was wearing that red heart necklace while she smiled into the camera.

Panic and fury tangled up inside him and tightened into a knot that made him feel like he was choking. He couldn't tear his gaze from the photo of the smiling little girl. "How does a man have a daughter and not know it?"

A daughter? How? What? Why? *Who?* He had a *child.* Judging by the picture, she looked to be four or five years old, so unless it was an old photo, there was only one woman who could be the girl's mother. And just like that, *the* woman was back, front and center in his mind.

How the hell had this happened? Stupid. He knew *how* it had happened. What he didn't know was why he hadn't been told. Wes rubbed one hand along the back of his neck and didn't even touch the tension building there. Still staring at the smiling girl on the screen, he felt the email batter away at his brain until he was forced to sit, open a new window and go to Twitter.

Somebody had hacked his account. His new handle was, as promised, Deadbeatdad. If he didn't get this stopped fast, it would go viral and might start interfering with his business.

Instantly, Wes made some calls, reporting that his account had been hacked, then turned the mess over to his IT guys to figure out. He reported the hack and had the account shuttered, hoping to buy time. Meanwhile, he was too late to stop #Deadbeatdad from spreading. The Twitterverse was already moving on it. Now he had a child he had to find and a reputation he had to repair. Snatching up the phone, he stabbed the button for his assistant's desk. "Robin," he snapped. "Get Mike from PR back in here *now*."

He didn't even wait to hear her response, just slammed the phone down and went back to his computer. He brought up the image of the little girl—his *daughter*—again and stared at her. What was her name? Where did she live? Then thoughts of the woman who had to be the girl's mother settled into his brain. Isabelle Gray. She'd disappeared from his life years ago—apparently with his child. Jaw tight, eyes narrowed, Wes promised himself he was going to get to the bottom of all of this and when he did…

For the next hour, everyone in PR and IT worked the situation. There was no stopping the flood of retweets, so Wes had Mike and his crew focused on finding a way to spin it. IT was tasked with tracking down this mysterious Maverick so that Wes could deal with him head-on.

Meanwhile, Wes had another problem to worry about. The merger with PlayCo, a major player in the toy industry, was something Wes had been carefully maneuvering his way toward for months. But the CEO there, Teddy Bradford, was a good old boy with rock-solid claims to family values. He'd been married to the same woman forever, had several kids and prided himself on being the flag bearer for the all-American, apple pie lifestyle.

This was going to throw a wrench of gigantic proportions into the mix. And so far, Teddy wasn't taking any of Wes's calls. Not a good sign.

"Uh, boss?"

"Yeah?" Wes spun around to look at one of the PR grunts. What the hell was her name? Stacy? Tracy? "What is it?"

"Teddy Bradford is holding a press conference. The news channel's website is running it live."

He stalked to her desk and only vaguely noticed that the others in the room had formed a half circle behind him. They were all watching as Bradford stepped up to a microphone and held his hands out in a settle-down gesture. As soon as he had quiet, he said, "After the disturbing revelations on social media this afternoon, I'm here to announce that I will be taking a step back to reevaluate my options before going through with the much anticipated merger."

Wes ground his teeth together and fisted his hands at his sides. Teddy could play it any way he wanted to for the press, but it was easy to see the merger was, at the moment, dead. All around him, his employees took a collective breath that sounded like a gasp.

But Teddy wasn't finished. The older man looked somber, sad, but Wes was pretty sure he caught a gleam of satisfaction in the other man's eyes. Hell, he was probably enjoying this. Nothing the man liked better than sitting high on his righteous horse. Teddy hadn't even bothered to take his call, preferring instead to call a damn press conference. Bastard.

"Here at PlayCo," Teddy was saying, "we put a high priority on family values. In fact, you could say that's the dominant trademark of my company and it always will be. A man's family is all important—or should be. After this morning's revelations, I have to say that clearly, Wes Jackson is not the man I'd believed him to be, and so I have some thinking to do in the next few days. As things stand now, it would take a miracle to persuade me to believe otherwise." Questions were fired at him, cameras chattered as shutters clicked over and over again. But Teddy was done.

"That's it. That's all I've got to say." He looked out over the crowd. "You have more questions, I suggest you throw them at Wes Jackson. Good day." He left the podium in the midst of a media circus and Wes rubbed his eyes, trying to ease the headache crouched behind them.

Stacy/Tracy turned the sound off on the computer, and silence dropped over everyone in the room like a damn shroud. Inside Wes, irritation bubbled into anger and then morphed quickly into helpless rage.

There was nowhere to turn it. Nowhere to focus it and get any kind of satisfaction.

As of now, the merger was in the toilet. And yeah, he was concentrating on the business aspect of this nightmare because he didn't have enough information to concentrate on the personal. Furious, Wes watched his PR team scramble to somehow mitigate the growing disaster. His assistant was already fielding calls from the media and this story seemed to be growing by the minute. Nothing people liked better than a scandal, and whoever this Maverick was, they obviously knew it.

For the first time ever, Wes felt helpless, and he didn't like it. Not only was his company taking a hit, but somewhere out there, he had a child he'd known nothing about. How the hell had this Maverick discovered the girl? Was Isabelle in on all of this? Or was someone close to her hoping for a giant payout along with pay*back*? Whatever the reason, this attack was deliberate. Someone had arranged a deliberate assault on him and his company. That someone was out to ruin him, and his brain worked feverishly trying to figure out just who was behind it all.

Running a successful business meant that you would naturally make enemies. But until today he wouldn't have thought that any of them would stoop to something like this. So he went deeper, beyond business and into the personal, looking for anyone who might have set him up for a fall like this. And only one name rose up in his mind. His ex-girlfriend, Cecelia Morgan.

She and Belle had been friendly for a while back in the day. Maybe Cecelia had known about the baby. Maybe she was the one who had started all this. Hell, she might even be Maverick herself. Cecelia hadn't taken it well when he broke up with her, and God knew she had a vicious temper. But if she was behind it all, *why*? Her company, To the Moon, sold upscale merchandise for kids. They weren't in direct competition, but she was as devoted to her business as Wes was to his, and maybe that was the main reason the two of them hadn't worked out. Or, he told himself, maybe it was the mean streak he'd witnessed whenever Cecelia was with her two best friends, Simone Parker and Naomi Price. He knew for a fact that people in Royal called the three women the Mean Girls. They were rich, beautiful, entitled and sometimes not real careful about the things they said to and about people.

He didn't know if she'd had anything to do with what was happening, but there was one sure way to find out. Leaving his employees scrambling, Wes drove home to Royal to confront his ex and, just maybe, get some answers. The drive did nothing to calm him down, since his brain kept focusing on the photo of that little girl. His daughter, for God's sake.

He needed answers. The only one who could give them to him was Belle, so finding her was priority one. His IT staff was now focused on not only mitigating his business disaster, but also in finding Isabelle Gray. But until he did locate Belle, Wes told himself, at least he could do *something*. Knowing

Cecelia could always be found at the Texas Cattleman's Club for lunch, he headed there the moment he hit town.

Cecelia was in the middle of what looked like a lunch meeting with a few of her employees. And though breaking it up would only encourage gossip, Wes wasn't interested in waiting for her to finish. The TCC was a legend in Royal, Texas. A members-only club, it had been around forever and only in the last several years had started accepting women as members—quite a few of the old guard still weren't happy about it. The dining room was elegant, understated and quiet but for the hush of conversation and the subtle clink of silverware against china.

On the drive from Houston, Wes's mind had raced with the implications of everything that had happened. A child he didn't know about. A merger in the toilet. His reputation shattered. And at the bottom of it all, maybe a vengeful ex. By the time he stood outside that dining room, he was ready for a battle.

"Mr. Jackson." The maître d' stepped up. "May I show you to a table? Are you alone for lunch or expecting guests?"

"Neither, thanks," Wes said, ignoring the man after a brief, polite nod. Wes speared Cecelia with a cold, hard gaze that caught her attention even from across the room. "I just need a word with Ms. Morgan."

Once she met his cool stare, she frowned slightly, then excused herself from the table and walked toward him. She was a gorgeous woman, and in a purely male response, Wes had to admire her even as his anger bubbled and churned inside. Her long, wavy blond hair lay across her shoulders and her gray-green eyes fixed on him, curiosity shining there. She wasn't very tall, but her generous figure and signature pout had brought more than one man in Texas to his knees.

She gave him a smile, then leaned in as if to kiss his cheek, but Wes pulled back out of reach. He caught the surprise and the insult in her eyes, but he only said, "We need to talk."

There were already enough people talking about his business today, so he took her forearm in a tight grip and led her away from the dining room to a quiet corner, hoping for at least a semblance of privacy. Cecelia pulled free as soon as he stopped and hissed, "What is going on with you?"

"You know damn well what," he said in a gravelly whisper. "That email you sent."

Those big, beautiful eyes clouded with confusion. "I have zero idea what you're talking about."

He studied her for a long minute, deciding whether she was lying or not. God knew he couldn't be sure, but he was going with instinct here. She didn't look satisfied with a mission accomplished. She looked irritated and baffled.

"Fine," he said grimly and dug his cell phone out of a pocket. Pulling up his email, he handed the phone to her and waited while she read it.

"Maverick? Who the heck is Maverick?"

Her expression read confusion and a part of him eased back a little. But if she wasn't Maverick, who was?

"Good question. I got an email this morning from a stranger. They sent me a picture of a daughter I never knew existed." He opened the attachment and showed her the picture of the smiling little girl. That's when he saw the flash of recognition in her eyes and he realized that Cecelia knew more than she was saying. Her face was too easy to read. His daughter's existence hadn't surprised her a bit.

"You knew about the girl." It wasn't a question. His chest felt tight.

Taking a deep breath, Cecelia blew out a breath and said, "I knew she was pregnant when she left. I didn't know she'd had a girl."

"She?"

Cecelia huffed out a breath. "Isabelle."

He swayed in place. He'd known it. Seeing that necklace on a little girl with his eyes had been impossible to deny. Isabelle. The woman he'd been involved with for almost a year had been pregnant with *his* daughter and hadn't bothered to tell him. More than that, though, was the fact that apparently Cecelia had known about his child, too, and kept the secret. Belle had left town. Cecelia had been right here in Royal. Seeing him all the damn time. And never once had she let on that he had a child out there. He couldn't rage at Belle. Yet. So it was the woman in front of him who got the full blast of what he was feeling. Every time she'd seen him for the last five years, she'd lied to him by not saying anything. She'd *known* he was a father and never said a damn word. What the hell? And who was Maverick and how did he know?

"You knew and didn't say anything?" His voice was low and tight.

She tossed a glance over her shoulder toward the table where she'd left her friends, then looked back at him. "No, I didn't. What would have been the point?"

He glared at her. "The point? My kid would be the point. And the fact that I didn't even know she existed."

"Please, Wes. How many times have you said you don't want kids or a family or anything remotely resembling commitment?"

"Not important."

"Yeah, it is." She was getting defensive—he heard it in her voice. "She was pretty sure you wouldn't be happy about the baby and I agreed. I just told her what you'd said so many times—that you weren't interested in families or forever."

Having his own words thrown back at him stung, but worse was the fact that *two* women he'd been with had conspired to keep his child from him. No, he'd never planned on kids or a wife, but that didn't mean he wouldn't want to know.

"Then what?" he asked, his voice sounding as if it was scraping along shattered glass. "You wait a few years, find this Maverick and tell *him*? Help him slam me across social media? For what? Payback?"

Her head snapped back and her eyes went even wider. "I would never do that to you, Wes," she said, and damned if he didn't almost believe her. "I wouldn't hurt you like that."

"Yeah?" he countered. "Your rep says otherwise."

She flushed and took a deep breath. "Believe what you want, but it wasn't me."

"Fine. Then where is Isabelle?"

"I don't know. She only said she was going home. A small town in Colorado. Swan…something. I forget. Honestly, we haven't stayed in touch." Tentatively, she reached out one hand and laid it on his forearm. "But I'll help you look for her."

"You helped enough five years ago," Wes ground out, and saw her reaction to the harsh tone flash in her eyes.

Too bad. He didn't have time to worry about insulting a woman who very well might be at the heart of this Maverick business. Sure, she claimed innocence, but he'd be a fool to take her word for it. When he rushed out, he barely noticed the waiter hovering nearby.

Wes's entire IT department was working on this problem, but he should be researching himself. His own tech skills were more than decent. He could have found Isabelle years ago, if he'd been looking. Yeah, he'd have to sift through a lot of information on the web, but he'd find her.

And when he did, heaven better help her, because hell would be dropping onto her doorstep.

Isabelle Graystone sat at the kitchen table working with a pad and pen while her daughter enjoyed her post-preschool snack.

"Mommy," Caroline said, her fingers dancing as she spoke, "can I have more cookies?"

Isabelle looked at the tiny love of her life and smiled. At four years old, Caroline was beautiful, bright, curious and quite the con artist when it came to getting more cookies. That sly smile and shy glance did it every time.

Isabelle's hands moved in sign language as she said, "Two more and that's it."

Caroline grinned and helped herself. Her heels tapped against the rungs of the kitchen chair as she cupped both hands around her glass of milk to take a sip.

Watching her, Isabelle smiled thoughtfully. It wasn't easy for a child to be different, but Caroline had such a strong personality that wearing hearing aids didn't bother her in the least. And learning to sign had opened up her conversational skills. Progressive hearing loss would march on, though, Isabelle knew, and one day her daughter would be completely deaf.

So Isabelle was determined to do everything she could to make her little girl's life as normal as possible. Which might also include a cochlear implant at some point. She wasn't there yet, but she was considering all of her options. There was simply nothing she wouldn't do for Caroline.

"After lunch," Isabelle said, "I have to go into town. See some people about the fund-raiser party I'm planning. Do you want to come with me, or stay here with Edna?"

Chewing enthusiastically, Caroline didn't speak,

just used sign language to say, "I'll come with you. Can we have ice cream, too?"

Laughing, Isabelle shook her head. "Where are you putting all of this food?"

A shrug and a grin were her only answers. Then the doorbell rang and Isabelle said, "Someone's at the door. You finish your cookies."

She walked through the house, hearing the soft click of her own heels against the polished wood floors. There were landscapes hanging on the walls, and watery winter sunlight filtering through the skylight positioned over the hallway. It was an elegant but homey place, in spite of its size. The restored Victorian stood on three acres outside the small town of Swan Hollow, Colorado.

Isabelle had been born and raised there, and when she'd found herself alone and pregnant, she'd come running back to the place that held her heart. She hadn't regretted it, either. It was good to be in a familiar place, nice knowing that her daughter would have the same memories of growing up in the forest that she did, and then there was the added plus of having her three older brothers nearby. Chance, Eli and Tyler were terrific uncles to Caroline and always there for Isabelle when she needed them—and sometimes when she didn't. The three of them were still as protective as they'd been when she was just a girl—and though it could get annoying on occasion, she was grateful for them, too.

Shaking her long, blond hair back from her face, she opened the door with a welcoming smile on her face—only to have it freeze up and die. A ball of ice dropped into the pit of her stomach even as her heartbeat jumped into overdrive.

Wes Jackson. The one man she'd never thought to see again. The one man she still dreamed of almost every night. The one man she could never forget.

"Hello, Belle," he said, his eyes as cold and distant as the moon. "Aren't you going to invite me in?"

Two

Isabelle felt her heart lurch to a stop then kick to life again in a hard thump. *Invite him in?* What she wanted to do was step back inside, slam the door and lock it. Too bad she couldn't seem to move. She did manage to choke out a single word. "Wes?"

"So you do remember me. Good to know." He moved in closer and Isabelle instinctively took a step back, pulling the half-open door closer, like a shield.

Panic nibbled at her, and Isabelle knew that in a couple more seconds it would start taking huge, gobbling bites. As unexpected as it was to find Wes Jackson standing on her front porch, there was a part of her that wasn't the least bit surprised to see him. Somehow, she'd half expected that one day, her past would catch up to her.

It had been five long years since she'd seen him, yet looking at him now, it could have been yesterday. Even in this situation, with his eyes flashing fury, she felt that bone-deep stir of something hot and needy and oh, so tempting. What was *wrong* with her? Hadn't she learned her lesson?

Isabelle had loved working for Texas Toys. They were open to new ideas and Wes had been the kind of boss everyone should have. He encouraged his employees to try new and different things and rewarded hard work. He was always hands-on when it came to introducing fresh products to his established line. So he and Isabelle had worked closely together as she came up with new toys, new designs. When she'd given in to temptation, surrendered to the heat simmering between them, Isabelle had known that it wouldn't end well. Boss/employee flings were practically a cliché after all. But the more time she spent with him, the more she'd felt for him until she'd made the mistake of falling in love with him.

That's when everything had ended. When he'd told her that he wasn't interested in more than an affair. He'd broken her heart, and when she left Texas, she'd vowed to never go back.

It seemed though, she hadn't had to. Texas had come to *her*.

"We have to talk." His voice was clipped, cold.

"No, we really don't." Isabelle wasn't going to give an inch. She wasn't even sure why he was here, and if he didn't know the whole truth, she wasn't going to give him any information. The only important thing was getting rid of him before he could see Caroline.

"That's not gonna fly," he said and moved in, putting both hands on her shoulders to ease her back and out of the way.

The move caught her so off guard, Isabelle didn't even try to hold her ground. He was already walking into the house before she could stop him. And even as she opened her mouth to protest, his arm brushed against her breast and she shivered. It wasn't fear stirring inside her, not even panic. It was desire.

The same flush of need had happened to her years ago whenever Wes was near. Almost from the first minute she'd met him, that jolt of something *more* had erupted between them. She'd never felt anything like it before Wes—or since. Of course, since she came back home to Swan Hollow, she hadn't exactly been drowning in men.

After Wes, she'd made the decision to step back from relationships entirely. Instead, she had focused on building a new life for her and her daughter. And especially during the last year or so, that focus had shut out everything else. Isabelle had her brothers, her daughter, and she didn't need anything else. Least of all the man who'd stolen her heart only to crush it underfoot.

With those thoughts racing through her mind, she closed the door and turned to face her past.

"I think I deserve an explanation," he said tightly.

"You *deserve*?" she repeated, in little more than a hiss. She shot a quick look down the hall toward the kitchen where Caroline was. "Really? That's what you want to lead with?"

"You should have told me about our daughter."

Shock slapped at her. But at the same time, a tiny voice in the back of Isabelle's mind whispered, *Of course he knows. Why else would he be here?* But how had he found out?

One dark eyebrow lifted. "Surprised? Yeah, I can see that. Since you've spent *five years* hiding the truth from me."

Hard to argue with that, since he was absolutely right. But on the other hand… "Wes—"

He held up one hand and she instantly fell into silence even though she was infuriated at herself for reacting as he expected her to.

"Spare me your excuses. There *is* no excuse for this. Damn it, Isabelle, I had a right to know."

Okay, that was enough to jolt her out of whatever fugue state he'd thrown her into. Keeping her voice low, she argued, "A right? I should have told you about *my* daughter when you made it perfectly clear you had no interest in being a father?"

Wanting to get him out of the hall where Caroline might see him, she walked past him into the living room. It was washed with pale sunlight, even on this gloomy winter day. The walls were a pale green and dotted with paintings of forests and sunsets and oceans. There were books lining the waist-high bookcases that ran the perimeter of the room and several comfortable oversize chairs and couches.

Oak tables were scattered throughout and a blue

marble-tiled hearth was filled with a simmering fire. This room—heck, this *house*—was her haven. She'd made a home here for her and Caroline. It was warm and cozy in spite of its enormous size, and she loved everything about it. So why was it, she wondered, that with Wes Jackson standing in the cavernous room, she suddenly felt claustrophobic?

He came up right behind her and she felt as if she couldn't draw a breath. She wanted him out. Now. Before Caroline could come in and start asking questions Isabelle didn't want to answer. She whipped around to face him, to finish this, to allow him to satisfy whatever egotistical motive had brought him here so he could leave.

His aqua eyes were still so deep. So mesmerizing. Even with banked anger glittering there, she felt drawn to him. And that was just…sad. His collar-length blond hair was ruffled, as if he'd been impatiently driving his fingers through it. His jaw was set and his mouth a firm, grim line. This was the face he regularly showed the world. The cool, hard businessman with an extremely low threshold for lies.

But she'd known the real man. At least, she'd told herself at the time that the man she talked, laughed and slept with was the real Wes Jackson. When they were alone, his guard was relaxed, though even then, she'd had to admit that he'd held a part of himself back. Behind a wall of caution she hadn't been able to completely breach. She'd known even then that Wes would continue to keep her at a safe distance and though it had broken her heart to acknowledge it, for her own sake, and the sake of her unborn child, she'd had to walk away.

"That was a hypothetical child," he ground out, and every word sounded harsh, as if it was scraping against his throat. "I never said I wouldn't want a child who was already *here*."

A tiny flicker of guilt jumped into life in the center of her chest, but Isabelle instantly smothered it. Five years ago, Wes had made it clear he wasn't interested in a family. He'd told her in no uncertain terms that he didn't want a wife. Children. *Love.* She'd left. Come home. Had her baby alone, with her three older brothers there to support her. Now Caroline was happy, loved, settled. How was Isabelle supposed to feel guilty about doing the best thing for her child?

So she stiffened her spine, lifted her chin and met Wes's angry glare with one of her own. "You won't make me feel bad about a decision I made in the best interests of my daughter."

"*Our* daughter, and you had no right to keep her from me." He shoved both hands into the pockets of his black leather jacket, then pulled them free again. "Damn it, Isabelle, you didn't make that baby on your own."

"No, I didn't," she said, nodding. "But I've taken care of her on my own. Raised her on my own. You don't get to storm into my life and start throwing orders around, Wes. I don't work for you anymore, and this is *my* home."

His beautiful eyes narrowed on her. "You lied to me. For five years, you lied to me."

"I haven't even spoken to you."

"A lie of omission is still a lie," he snapped.

He was right, but she had to wonder. Was he here because of the child he'd just discovered or because she'd wounded his pride? She tipped her head to one side and studied him. "You haven't even asked where she is, or how she is. Or even what her name is. This isn't about her for you, Wes. This is about *you*. Your ego."

"Her name is Caroline," he said softly. He choked out a laugh that never reached his eyes. "I'm pretty good at research myself. You know, you're something else." Shaking his head he glanced around the room before skewering her with another hard look. "You think this is about ego? You took off. With *my* kid—and never bothered to tell me."

Was it just outrage she was hearing? Or was there pain in his voice as well? Hard to tell when Wes spent his life hiding what he was feeling, what he was thinking. Even when she had been closest to him, she'd had to guess what was going through his mind at any given moment. Now was no different.

She threw another worried glance toward the open doorway. Time was ticking past, and soon Caroline would come looking for her. Edna, the housekeeper, would be home from the grocery store soon, and frankly, Isabelle wanted Wes gone before she was forced to answer any questions about him.

"How did you find out?" she asked abruptly, pushing aside the guilt he kept trying to pile on her.

He scraped one hand across his face then pushed that hand through his hair, letting her know that whatever he was feeling was in turmoil. Isabelle hadn't known he was capable of this kind of emotion. She didn't know whether she was pleased or worried.

"You haven't seen the internet headlines today?"

"No." Worry curled into a ball in the pit of her stomach and twisted tightly. "What's happened?"

"Someone knew about our daughter. And they've been hammering me with that knowledge."

"How?" She glanced at her laptop and thought briefly about turning it on, catching up with what was happening. But the easiest way to discover what she needed to know was to hear it directly from Wes.

"I got an email yesterday from someone calling themselves Maverick. Sent me a picture of my daughter."

"How did you know she was yours?"

He gave her a cool look. "She was wearing the princess heart necklace I once gave you."

Isabelle sighed a little and closed her eyes briefly. "She loves that necklace." Caro had appropriated the plastic piece of jewelry, and seeing it on her daughter helped Belle push the memory of receiving it from Wes into the background.

"You liked it once too, as I remember."

Her gaze shot up to his. "I used to like a lot of things."

Nodding at that jab, Wes said, "The same person

who sent me the picture also let me know my Twitter account had been hacked. Whoever it was gave me a new handle. Real catchy. Deadbeatdad."

"Oh, God."

"Yeah, that pretty much sums it up." He shook his head again. "That new hashtag went viral so fast my IT department couldn't contain it. Before long, reporters were calling, digging for information. Then Teddy Bradford at PlayCo called a press conference to announce the merger we had planned was now up in the air because, apparently," he muttered darkly, "I'm too unsavory a character to be aligned with his family values company."

"Oh, no..." Isabelle's mind was racing. Press conferences. Reporters. Wes Jackson was big news. Not just because of his toy company, but because he was rich, handsome, a larger-than-life Texas tycoon who made news wherever he went. And with the interest in him, that meant that his personal life was fodder for stories. Reporters would be combing through Wes's past. They would find Caroline. They would do stories, take pictures and, in general, open her life up to the world. This was fast becoming a nightmare.

"The media's been hounding me since this broke. I've got Robin fielding calls—she'll stonewall them for as long as she can."

Wes's assistant was fierce enough to hold the hordes at bay—but it wouldn't last. They would eventually find her. Find Caroline. But even as threads of panic unwound and spiraled through her veins, Isabelle was already trying to figure out ways to protect her daughter from the inevitable media onslaught.

"So." Wes got her attention again. "More lies. You're not Isabelle *Gray*. Your real last name is Graystone. Imagine my surprise when I discovered *that*. Isabelle Gray didn't leave much of a mark on the world—but while typing in the name you gave me, up popped Isabelle *Graystone*. And a picture of you. So yeah. Surprised. Even more surprised to find out your family is all over the business world. As in Graystone shipping. Graystone hotels. Graystone every damn thing.

"You didn't tell me you were rich. Didn't tell me your family has their fingers into every known pie in the damn country. You didn't even tell me your damn name. You lied," he continued wryly. "But then, you seem to be pretty good at that."

She flushed in spite of everything as she watched his gaze slide around the room before turning back to her. Fine, she had lied. But she'd done what she'd had to, so she wouldn't apologize for it. And while that thought settled firmly into her brain, Isabelle ignored the niggle of guilt that continued to ping inside her.

"Why'd you hide who you were when you were working for me?"

Isabelle blew out a breath and said, "Because I wanted to be hired for *me*, for what I could do. Not because of who my family is."

Irritation, then grudging respect flashed across his face. "Okay. I can give you that one."

"Well," she said, sarcasm dripping in her tone. "Thank you so much."

He went on as if she hadn't said a word. "But once you had the job, you kept up the lie." His eyes narrowed on her. "When we were sleeping together, you were still lying to me."

"Only about my name." She wrapped her arms around her middle and held on. "I couldn't tell you my real name without admitting that I'd lied to get the job."

"A series of lies, then," he mused darkly. "And the hits just keep on coming."

"Why are you even here, Wes?" She was on marked time here and she knew it. Though it felt as if time was crawling past, she and Wes had already been talking for at least ten minutes. Caroline could come into the room any second. And Isabelle wasn't ready to have *that* conversation with her little girl.

"You can even ask me that?" he said, astonishment clear in his tone. "I just found out I'm a father. I'm here to see my daughter."

Damn it. "That's not a good idea."

"Didn't think you'd like it." He nodded sharply. "Good thing it's not up to you."

"Oh, yes, it is," Isabelle said, lifting her chin to meet his quiet fury with some of her own.

Funny, she'd thought about what this moment might be like over the years. How she would handle it if and when Wes discovered he had a child. She'd wondered if he'd even *care*. Well, that question had been answered. At least, partially. He cared.

But what was it that bothered him most? That he had a child he didn't know? Or that Isabelle had lied to him? At the moment, it didn't matter.

"You don't want to fight me on this, Belle." He took a step closer and stopped. "She's my daughter, isn't she?"

No point in trying to deny it, since once he saw Caroline, all doubts would disappear. The girl looked so much like her dad, it was remarkable. "Yes."

He nodded, as if absorbing a blow. "Thanks for not lying about it this time."

"Wes..."

"I have the right to meet her. To get to know her. To let her know me." He stalked to the fireplace, laid one hand on the mantel and stared into the flames. "What does she know about me?" He turned his head to look at her. "What did you tell her?"

His eyes were gleaming, his jaw was set and every line of his body radiated tension and barely controlled anger.

"I told her that her father couldn't be with us but that he loved her."

He snorted. "Well, thanks for that much, anyway."

"It wasn't for your benefit," she said flatly. "I don't want my daughter guessing that her father didn't want her."

"I would have," he argued, pushing away from the mantel to face her again. "If I'd known."

"Easy enough to say now."

"Well, I guess we'll never know if things would have been different, will we?" he said tightly. "But from here on out, Belle, things are going to change. I'm not going anywhere. I'm in this. She's mine and I want to be part of her life."

Isabelle was so caught up in the tension strung between them, she almost didn't notice Caroline walk quietly into the room to stand beside her. Her first instinct was to stand in front of her. To somehow hide the little girl from the father who had finally found her. But it was far too late for that.

Instantly, Wes's gaze dropped to the girl, and his features softened, the ice melted from his eyes and a look of wonder crossed his face briefly. Of course he could see the resemblance. Isabelle saw it every time she looked at her daughter. She was a tiny, feminine version of Wes Jackson and there was just no way he could miss it.

"Hi," he said, his voice filled with a warmth that had been lacking since the moment he arrived.

"Hi," Caroline said, as her fingers flew. "Who are you?"

Before he could say anything, Isabelle said, "This is Mr. Jackson, sweetie. He's just leaving in a minute."

He shot her one quick, hard look, as Isabelle dropped one hand protectively on her daughter's shoulder.

"We're not done talking." His gaze was hard and cold, his voice hardly more than a hush of sound.

"I guess not," she said, then looked down at her baby girl. Using her hands as well as her voice, she said, "I heard Edna's car pull into the driveway a minute ago. Why don't you go help her with the groceries? Then you can go upstairs and play while Mommy talks to the man."

"What about the ice cream?" Caro asked.

"Later," she signed. Sighing a little, she watched Caroline smile and wave at Wes before turning to head back to the kitchen.

Once the little girl had hurried out of the room, Wes looked at Isabelle. "She's deaf?"

"Good catch," she said and instantly regretted the sarcasm. No point in antagonizing the man any further than he already was. "Yes. She has progressive hearing loss."

"And what does that mean exactly? For her?"

"That's a long conversation better suited to another time," Isabelle said, in no mood whatsoever to get into this with Wes right this minute.

She wouldn't have thought it possible, but his features went even icier. "Fine. We'll put that aside for now." He lowered his voice. "You should have told me. About her. About everything."

Fresh guilt rushed through her like floodwaters spilling over a dam, but she fought it back. Yes, she remembered what it had been like to discover that Caroline was losing her hearing. The panic. The fear. The completely helpless feelings that had swamped her for days. Now she could look into Wes's eyes and see the same reactions she'd once lived through. He had been hit with a lot of information in a very short time, and if it had been her, she probably wouldn't have been as controlled as he was managing to be.

For some reason, that really irritated her.

Isabelle was willing to live with the consequences of the decision she'd made so long ago. Besides, in spite of being faced with Wes now, she was still sure that not telling him had been the right choice. "I did what I thought was right, Wes. You more than anyone should appreciate that."

"What's that supposed to mean?"

"Oh, please." She laughed shortly and wished tears weren't starting to pool behind her eyes. "You go through life making split-second decisions. You trust your gut. And you go with it. That's all I did, and I'm not going to apologize for it now."

He moved in on her until she swore she could feel heat radiating from his body and reaching out to hers. She caught his scent and helplessly dragged it into her lungs, savoring the taste of him even as she knew that going down this road again would lead to nothing but misery.

Besides, she reminded herself wryly, that wasn't passion glittering in his eyes. It was fury.

"We're not done here, Belle."

She gulped a breath, but it didn't help the sudden jolt to her heart. No one but Wes had ever called her Belle, and just hearing him say it again brought her back to long nights on silk sheets, wrapped in his arms. Why was it that she could still feel the rush of desire after so long? And why *now*, for heaven's sake?

It had taken her years to get past those memories, to train herself to never relive them. To push her time in Texas so far back in her mind that she could almost believe it never happened. Until she looked into her baby girl's face and saw the man she couldn't forget.

"I can't talk about this now. Not with Caroline here. I don't want her—"

"Informed?" he asked. "Can't take the chance of her finding out her father is here and wants to be with her?"

"It's a lot to put on a little girl, Wes, and I'm not going to dump it all on her until you and I come to some sort of agreement."

"What kind of agreement?" His tone was cautious. Suspicious.

"Like I said, not here." She took a breath to steady herself and wasn't even surprised when it didn't work. How could she find her balance when staring into the aqua eyes that had haunted her dreams for years? "Once you get back to Texas, call me and we'll talk everything out."

A half smile curved his mouth then disappeared, leaving no trace behind. "I'm not going back to Texas. Not yet."

"What? Why? What?" Her brain short-circuited. It was the only explanation for the way she was stumbling for words and coming up empty.

"I've got a room at the Swan Hollow Palace hotel," he said. "I'm not going anywhere until I get some time with my daughter. So that agreement you want to work on? We'll be doing it here. Up close and personal."

Her heart was racing, and breathing was becoming an issue. As if he could read exactly what she was thinking, feeling, he gave her that cold, calculated smile again, and this time, Isabelle's stomach sank.

"What time does she go to bed?"

"What?" God, she sounded like an idiot. "Eight o'clock. Why?"

"Because I'll be here at eight thirty." He headed out of the room, but paused at the threshold and looked back at her. Eyes fixed on hers he said, "Be ready to talk. I'm staying, Belle. For as long as this takes, I'm staying. I'm going to get to know my daughter. I'm going to catch up on everything I've missed. And there's not a damn thing you can do about it."

Swan Hollow, Colorado, was about thirty miles southwest of Denver and as different from that bustling city as it was possible to be. The small town was upscale but still clearly proud of its Western roots.

Tourists, skiers and snowboarders visited and shopped at the boutiques, antique stores and art galleries. Main Street was crowded with cafés, restaurants, bars and a couple of B&Bs, along with the shops. There was even a small mom-and-pop grocery store for those who didn't want to make the drive to the city.

The buildings on Main Street were huddled close together, some with brick facades, others with wood fronts deliberately made to look weather-beaten. Tall iron streetlamps lined the sidewalks and gave the impression of old-fashioned gas lights. Baskets of winter pines with tiny white lights strung through their branches hung from every lamppost. Every parking spot along the street was taken, and hordes of people hustled along the sidewalks, moving in and out of shops, juggling bags and exhaling tiny fogs of vapor into the air.

If he were here on vacation, Wes might have been charmed by the place. As it was, though, his mind was too busy to pay much attention to his surroundings. Amazing how a man's world could crash and burn within forty-eight hours.

The Palace hotel stood on a corner of Main Street, its brick facade, verdigris-tinged copper trim and shining windows making a hell of a statement. He'd already been told by the hotel clerk that the place had been in business since 1870. It had had plenty of face-lifts over the years, of course, but still managed to hold onto its historic character, so that stepping into the hotel was like moving into a time warp.

He walked into the lobby, with its scarlet rugs spread out across gleaming wood floors. Cream-colored walls were decorated with paintings by local artists, celebrating the town's mining history and the splendor of the mountains that encircled Swan Hollow on three sides. The lobby was wide and warm, with wood trim, a roaring fire in the stone hearth and dark red leather sofas and chairs sprinkled around the room, encouraging people to sit and enjoy themselves. He was greeted by muted conversations and the soft chime of an elevator bell as the car arrived.

The quiet, soothing atmosphere did nothing to ease the roiling tension within him.

He avoided eye contact with everyone else as he walked past the check-in desk, a long, shining slab of oak that looked as if it had been standing in that spot since the hotel first opened. Wes took the elevator to the top floor, then walked down the hall to his suite. After letting himself in, he shrugged out of his jacket, tossed it onto the dark blue couch and walked across the room to the French doors. He threw them open, stepped out onto his balcony and let the icy wind slap some damn sense into him.

January in Colorado was freezing. Probably beautiful, too, if you didn't have too much on your mind. There was snow everywhere and the pines looked like paintings, dripping with layers of snow that bowed their branches. People streamed up and down the sidewalks, but Wes ignored all that activity and lifted his gaze to the mountains beyond the town limits. Tall enough to scrape the sky, the tips of the mountains had low-hanging gray clouds hovering over them like fog.

Wes's hands fisted around the black iron railing in front of him, and the bite of cold gave him a hard jolt. Maybe he needed it. God knew he needed something.

He had a *daughter.* There was no denying the truth even if he wanted to—which he didn't. The little girl looked so much like him, anyone would see the resemblance. His child. His little girl.

His stomach twisted into knots as the enormity of this situation hit him. He huffed out a breath and watched the cloud of it dissipate in the cold air. That beautiful little girl was *his*. And she was deaf.

He should have *known*.

He should have been a part of all of this. He might have been able to do something—anything—to help. And even if he couldn't have, it was his *right* to be a part of it. To do his share of worrying. But his daughter's mother hadn't bothered to clue him in.

As furious as he was with Isabelle, as stunned as he was at being faced with a *daughter*, he couldn't deny it wasn't only anger he'd felt when he was in that house.

"She looks even better now than she did five years ago," he muttered. Isabelle had always had a great body, but now, since having a child, she was softer, rounder and damn near irresistible.

Instantly, her image appeared in his mind and the grip he had on the icy railing tightened until his knuckles went white. That long, blond hair, those eyes that were caught somewhere between blue and green, the mouth that could tempt a dead man. He hadn't seen her in five years and his body was burning for her.

"Which just goes to prove," he mumbled, "your brain's not getting enough of the blood flow."

He shivered as the wind slapped at him, and he finally gave up and walked back into his suite. With everything else going on, he didn't need a case of pneumonia. Closing the doors behind him, he went to the fireplace and flipped a switch to turn on the gas-powered flames.

It was quiet. Too damn quiet. He stared at the fire for a minute or two, then dropped onto the couch, propping his boots up on the sturdy coffee table. Late afternoon sunlight came through the windows in a pale stream, the fire burned, and his brain just shut down. He needed to think, but how the hell could he when he was distracted by his own body's reaction to the woman who'd lied to him since the moment he met her?

"Isabelle Gray." How had she managed to get hired under a false name? Didn't his damn personnel department do a better job of checking résumés than that? "And she's rich," he exclaimed to the empty room. "Why the hell was she working for me anyway?"

But the "rich" part probably explained how she'd gotten away with changing her name to get a job. She'd been able to pay for whatever she'd needed to adopt a different name. Closing his eyes, Wes remembered the slap of shock he'd felt when looking for Isabelle Gray online only to find Isabelle *Graystone.* The names were enough alike that the search engine had hooked onto her real identity. Seeing her picture, reading about who she really was had been yet another shock in a day already filled with them.

He had no explanation for any of this, and checking his watch, Wes saw that he had several hours before he could go back and demand she give him the answers he needed. What was he supposed to do until then?

He dragged his cell phone out of his pocket and

turned it back on. He'd had it off during his visit to Belle's house since he hadn't needed yet another distraction. Now, the message light blinked crazily and he scrolled through the list of missed calls.

Starting at the top, he hit speed dial and waited while his assistant's phone rang.

"Hi, boss," Robin said.

"Yeah, you called. Anything new?" He got up and walked to the bar in the far corner of the room. He opened the fridge, saw the complimentary cheese plate and helped himself before grabbing a beer. Twisting off the cap, he took a long drink to wash the cheese down and gave Robin his attention.

"IT department reports they're no closer to discovering who this Maverick is or even where he sent that email from."

"I thought they were supposed to be the best," he complained.

"Yeah, well, IT's pretty impressed with Maverick," she said wryly. "Seems he bounced his signal all over hell and back, so they're having a time pinning it down." She took a breath and said, "You already know that email account's been closed, so the guys here say there isn't much hope of running him to ground."

Perfect. He had his own computer experts and they couldn't give him a direction to focus the fury still clawing at his throat.

"What else?" Another swallow of beer as he plopped back onto the couch and stared at the flames dancing in the hearth.

"Personnel did a deeper check on the name you gave them, and turns out Isabelle Gray's name is really Graystone. Her family's got holdings in pretty much everything. She's an heiress."

He sighed. "Yeah, I know that."

"Oh. Well, that was anticlimactic. Okay. Moving on." She forced cheer into her voice. "On the upside, IT says the Twitter trend is dying off. Apparently you're down to number ten today instead of number one."

"Great." Wes made a mental note to check with his IT guys on the status of his Twitter account when he got off the phone. What he really needed was for some celebrity to do something shocking that would be enough to push him off the stage entirely.

"And the warehouses are set up for delivery of the doll. Everything's ready to roll out on time."

"Good." He set the beer on the coffee table and rubbed his eyes in a futile attempt to ease the headache pounding there. "Keep on top of this stuff, Robin, and make sure I'm in the loop."

"Boss," she said, "you *are* the loop."

He had to smile and he was grateful for it. "Right. Did you hear from Harry today?"

"Yep, he's on it. He's working with PR to put a spin on all this, and when he's got the ideas together, he says he'll call you to discuss it."

"Okay. Look, I'm going to be staying in Colorado for a while."

"How long?"

"Not sure yet." However long it took to make sure

the mother of his child understood that she was living in a new reality. "You can always get me on my cell. I'm at the Swan Hollow Palace hotel—"

"Swan Hollow?" she asked.

"Yeah." He smiled to himself again. "Weird name, but nice town from what I've seen."

"Good to know. I still can't believe you made the reservations yourself rather than let me handle it as always."

"I was in a hurry," Wes said and wondered why he was almost apologizing to his assistant for usurping her job.

She paused, then went on. "Fine, fine. When the final drawings on the PR campaign are turned in, I'll overnight them to you at the hotel. If you need anything else, let me know and I'll take care of it."

"Robin," he said with feeling, "you are the one bright spot in a fairly miserable couple of days."

"Thanks, boss," she said, and he heard the smile in her voice. "I'll remind you of that when I want a raise."

"I know you will," he said and was still smiling when he hung up.

Alone again, he drank his beer, and still facing hours to kill before speaking to Isabelle again, Wes had an idea. Grabbing the remote that worked both the flat-screen television and the computer, he turned the latter on. In a few minutes, he was watching an online video to learn ASL.

American Sign Language.

Three

Wes could have walked to Isabelle's house, since it was just outside town, but at night, the temperature dropped even farther and he figured he'd be an icicle by the time he arrived. The five-minute drive brought him to the long, winding road that stretched at least a half mile before ending in front of the stately Victorian. His headlights swept the front of the place and he took a moment to look it over.

The big house was painted forest green and boasted black shutters and white gingerbread trim. Surrounded as it was by snow-covered pines, the old house looked almost magical. Lamplight glowed from behind window glass, throwing golden shadows into the night. Porch lights shone from what used to be brass carriage lanterns and signaled welcome—

though Wes was fairly certain that welcome wasn't something Belle was feeling for him.

"Doesn't matter," he told himself. He turned off the engine and just sat there for a minute, looking up at the house. He'd been thinking about nothing but this moment for hours now, and he knew that this conversation would be the most important of his life. He had a child.

A daughter.

Just that thought alone was enough to make his insides jitter with nerves. He didn't even *know* her, yet he felt a connection to this child. There were so many different feelings running through him, he couldn't separate them all. Panic, of course—who could blame him for being terrified at the thought of being responsible for such a small human being? And whether Belle wanted to admit it or not, he *was* as responsible for Caroline as she was.

But there was more. There was…wonder. He'd helped to create a person. Okay, he hadn't had a clue, but that child was here. In the world. Because of *him*. He smiled to himself even as a fresh wave of trepidation rose up inside him.

Nothing in his life had worried him before this, but at least internally, Wes had to admit that being a father was a damn scary proposition. What the hell did he know about being a parent?

His own mother had died when Wes was six months old. His father, Henry Jackson, had raised him single-handedly. Henry had done a good job, but he'd also managed to let his son know in countless different ways that allowing a woman into your life was a sure path to misery. Though he'd made it clear it wasn't *having* a woman that was the problem—it was losing her.

He'd loved Wes's mother and was lost when she died. Once when Wes was sixteen, Henry had finally talked to him, warning him to guard his heart.

"Wes, you listen good. A woman's a fine thing for a man," Henry had mused, staring up at the wide, Texas sky on a warm summer night. "And finding one you can love more than your own life is a gift and a curse all at once."

"Why's that?" Wes held a sweating bottle of Coke between his palms and leaned back in the lawn chair beside his father. It had been a long, backbreaking day of work on the ranch, and Wes was exhausted. But he and his dad always ended the day like this, sitting out in the dark, talking, and it didn't even occur to him to give it up just because he was tired.

"Because once you give your heart to a woman, she can take it with her when she leaves." Henry turned and looked his son dead in the eye. "Your mama took mine when she died, and I've lived like half a man ever since."

Wes knew that to be true, since he'd seen the sorrow in his father's eyes ever since he was old enough to identify it.

"Love is a hard thing, Wes, and you just remember that, now that you're old enough to go sniffing around the females." He sighed and focused on the stars as if, Wes thought, the old man believed if he looked at the sky hard enough, he might be able to peer through the blackness and into Heaven itself.

"I'm not saying I regret a minute of loving your mother," Henry said on a heavy sigh. "Can't bring myself to say that, no matter how deep the loss of her cut me. Without her, I wouldn't have you, and I don't like the thought of that at all. What I'm trying to tell you, boy, is that it's better to not love too hard or too permanent. Easier to live your life when you're not worried about having the rug pulled out from under your feet." He stared into Wes's eyes. "Guard your heart, Wes. That's what I'm telling you."

Wes had listened well to his father's advice. Oh, he loved women. All women. But he kept them at arm's length, never letting them close enough to get beyond the wall he so carefully constructed around his heart. All through school, he'd been single-mindedly focused on building a business he started with his college roommate.

Together, they'd bought up hundreds of tiny, aerodynamically perfect toy planes at auction, then sold them at a profit to bored college students at UT. Within a week, planes had been flying from dorm windows, classrooms, down staircases. The students set up contests for flight, distance and accuracy. Seeing how quickly they'd sold out of their only product, Wes and his friend had put the money they made back into their growing business. Soon, they were the go-to guys for toys to help fight boredom and mental fatigue. By the time they graduated, Wes had found his life's path. He bought out his friend, allowing him to finance his way through medical school, and Wes took Texas Toy Goods Inc. to the top.

Along the way, there had been more women, but none of them had left a mark on him—until Belle. And he'd fought against that connection with everything he had. He wasn't looking for love. He'd seen his own father wallow in his sorrow until the day he died and was able to finally rejoin the woman he'd mourned for more than twenty years. Wes had no intention of allowing his life to be turned upside down for something as ephemeral as *love*.

Yet now here he was, out in front of Belle's house, where his *daughter* slept. The world as he knew it was over. The new world was undiscovered country. And, he told himself, there was no time like the present to start exploring it.

He got out of the car, turned the collar of his black leather jacket up against the wind, closed the car door and headed up the brick walk that had been shoveled clear. Funny to think about all the times he'd avoided the very complication he was now insisting on. Still, he thought as he climbed the steps to the porch, he could take the easy way out, go along with what Belle wanted and simply disappear. His daughter wouldn't miss him because she wasn't even aware of his existence.

And that was what gnawed at him. His little girl didn't know him. She'd looked up at him today and hadn't realized who the hell he was. Who would have thought that the simple action would have hit him so hard? So yeah, he could walk away, but what would that make him?

"A coward, that's what," he grumbled as he stood before the front door. Well, Wes Jackson was many things, but no one had ever accused him of cowardice, and that wasn't going to change now.

He might not have wanted children, but he had one now, and damned if he'd pretend otherwise. With that thought firmly in mind, he rapped his knuckles against the door and waited impatiently for it to open.

A second later, Belle was there, haloed in light, her blond hair shining, her eyes worried. She wore faded jeans and a long-sleeved, dark rose T-shirt. Her feet were bare and boasted bloodred polish on her nails.

Why he found that incredibly sexy, he couldn't have said and didn't want to consider.

"Is she asleep?" he asked.

"She's in bed," Belle answered. "Sleep is a separate issue." Stepping back to allow him to enter, she closed the door, locked it and said, "Usually, she lies awake for a while, talking to herself or to Lizzie."

Wes stopped in the act of shrugging out of his jacket and looked at her. "Who's Lizzie?"

"Her stuffed dog."

"Oh." Nodding, he took his jacket off and hung it on the coat tree beside the door. For a minute there he'd actually thought maybe he was the father of twins or something. Looking at Belle, he said, "I half expected you to not open the door to me tonight."

"I thought about it," she admitted, sliding her

hands into the pockets of her jeans. "Heck, I thought about snatching Caro up and flying to Europe. Just not being here when you showed up."

He hadn't considered that possibility. Now Wes realized he should have. He'd done his research and knew that Belle was wealthy enough to have disappeared if she'd wanted to, and he'd have spent years trying to find her and their daughter. Anger bubbled but was smoothed over by the fact that she hadn't run. That she was here. To give him the answers he needed.

"I would have found you."

"Yeah, I know." She pulled her hands free, then folded her arms across her chest and rubbed her upper arms briskly, as if she were cold. But the house was warm in spite of the frigid temperatures outside. So it must be nerves, he told himself and could almost sympathize. "That's just one of the reasons I didn't go."

Curious, he asked, "What're the others?"

Sighing a little, she looked up at him. "Believe it or not, you showing up here like this isn't the only thing I have to think about. My daughter comes first. I couldn't tear Caro away from her home. She has friends here. The uncles who love her are here. Secondly, this is my place, and I won't run. Not even from you."

He looked down into her eyes and saw pride and determination. He could understand that. Hell, he could *use* it. Her pride would demand that she listen to him whether she wanted to or not. Her pride would make sure she caved to his demands if only to prove she didn't fear him becoming a part of their daughter's life.

Belle had always been more complicated than any other woman he'd ever known. She was smart, funny, driven, and her personality was strong enough that she'd never had any trouble standing up for herself. Which meant that though he'd get his way in the end, it wouldn't be an easy road.

As they stood together in the quiet entryway, iron-clad pendant lights hung from the ceiling and cast shadows across her face that seemed to settle in her eyes. She looked...*vulnerable* for a second, and Wes steeled himself against feeling sympathy for her. Hell, she'd cheated him for five long years. He'd missed her pregnancy, missed the birth of his daughter, missed every damn thing. If anyone deserved some sympathy around here, it was *him*.

As if she could sense his thoughts, that vulnerability she'd inadvertently shown faded fast. "Do you want some coffee?"

"I want answers."

"Over coffee," she said. "Come on. We can sit in the kitchen."

He followed her down the hall, glancing around him as he went. The house was beautiful. There were brightly colored rugs spread everywhere on the oak floors so that the sound of his footsteps went from harsh to muffled as he navigated through the house. The dining room was big, but not formal. There was a huge pedestal table with six chairs drawn up to it.

Pine branches jutted up from a tall porcelain vase and spilled that rich fragrance into the air.

He couldn't help comparing her home to his own back in Royal. Though Wes's house was big and luxurious, it lacked the warmth he found here. Not surprising, he supposed, since he was only there to sleep and eat. The only other person who spent time in his house besides himself was his housekeeper, and she kept the place sparkling clean but couldn't do a thing about the impersonal feel. Frowning a little, he pushed those thoughts aside and focused on the moment at hand.

Isabelle didn't speak until they were in the kitchen, then it was only to say, "You still take your coffee black?"

"Yeah," he said, surprised she remembered. The kitchen had slate-blue walls, white cabinets, black granite on the counters and a long center island that boasted four stools. There was a small table with four chairs in a bay window, and Isabelle waved him toward it.

"Go sit down, this'll take a minute."

He took a chair that afforded him a view of her, and damned if he didn't enjoy it. He could be as angry as ever and still have a purely male appreciation for a woman who could look *that* good in jeans. Hell, maybe it was the Texan in him, but a woman who filled out denim like she did was the stuff dreams were made of. But he'd already had that dream and let it go, so there was no point in thinking about it again now.

He narrowed his gaze on her. She was nervous. He could see that, too.

Well, she had a right to be.

"So," he said abruptly, "how long have you lived here?"

She jolted a little at the sound of his voice reverberating through the big kitchen, but recovered quickly enough. Throwing him a quick glance, she set several cookies on a plate, then said, "In Swan Hollow? I grew up here."

He already knew that, thanks to the internet. "So you've always lived in this house?"

She took one mug out of the machine, reset it and set the next mug in place. "No, my brother Chance lives in the family home now."

One eyebrow lifted. Truth be told, as soon as he'd discovered who Belle was and where she lived, he hadn't looked any deeper. "You have a brother? Wait. Yeah. You said *uncles* earlier."

She gave him a wry smile. "I have three older brothers. Chance, Eli and Tyler. Fair warning, you'll probably be meeting them once they find out you're here."

Fine. He could handle her brothers. "They don't worry me."

"Okay. The three of them live just up the road. My parents had a big tract of land, and when they died, Chance moved into the big house and Eli and Tyler built homes for themselves on the land."

"Why didn't you? Why live here and not closer to your family?"

She laughed shortly. "In summer it takes about five minutes to walk to any of their houses. It's not like I'm far away." She carried a plate of cookies to the table and set them down. Homemade chocolate chip. When she turned to go back for the coffee, she said, "I wanted to live closer to town, with Caroline. She has school and friends…" Her voice trailed off as she set his coffee in front of him and then took her own cup and sat down in the chair opposite him.

"Big house for just the two of you," he mused, though even as he said it, he thought again about his own home. It was bigger than this place and only he and his housekeeper lived there.

"It's big, but when I was a girl, I loved this house." She looked around the kitchen and he knew she was seeing the character, the charm of the building, not the sleek appliances or the updated tile floor. "I used to walk past it all the time and wonder about what it was like inside. When it went up for sale, I had to have it. I had it remodeled and brought it back to life, and sometimes I think the house is grateful for it." She looked at him and shrugged. "Sounds silly, but…anyway, my housekeeper, Edna, and her husband, Marco, my gardener, live in the guest house out back. So Caro and I have the main house to ourselves."

Outside, the dark pressed against the windows, but the light in the room kept it at bay. Wes had a sip of coffee, more to take a moment to gather his thoughts than for anything else. He was at home in any situation, yet here and now, he felt a little off balance. It had started with his first look at Belle after five long years. Then seeing Caroline had just pushed him over the edge. He really hadn't taken in yet just how completely his life had been forever altered. All he knew for sure was that things were different now. And he had to forge a path through uncharted territory.

When he set the mug back on the table, he looked into her eyes and asked, "Did you tell Caroline who I am?"

She bit at her bottom lip. "No."

"Good."

"What?" Clearly surprised, she stared at him, questions in her eyes.

"I want her to get to know me before we spring it on her," Wes said. He'd had some time to think about this, during his long day of waiting, and though he wanted nothing more than to go upstairs and claim his daughter, it wasn't the smart plan. He wanted Caroline to get used to him, to come to like him before she found out he was her father.

"Okay," she said. "That makes sense, I guess."

She looked relieved and Wes spoke up fast to end whatever delusion she was playing out in her head. "Don't take this to mean I might change my mind about all of this. I'm not going anywhere. Caroline is *my* daughter, Belle. And I want her to know that. I'm going to be a part of her life, whether you like the idea or not."

Irritation flashed on her features briefly, then faded as she took a gulp of her coffee and set the mug down again. "I understand. But you have to understand something, too, Wes. I won't let Caroline be hurt."

Insult slapped at him. What was he, a monster? He wasn't looking to cause Caroline pain, for God's sake. He was her father and he wanted her to know that. "I'm not going to hurt her."

"Not intentionally. I know that," she said quickly. "But she's a little girl. She doesn't know how to guard her heart or to keep from becoming attached. If she gets used to having you around, having you be a part of her world, and then you back off, it will hurt her."

He was used to responsibility, but suddenly that feeling inched up several notches. Wes couldn't have a child and ignore her. But at the same time, he was about to break every rule he'd ever had about getting involved with someone. There was danger inherent in caring about anyone, and he knew it. But she was his daughter, and that single fact trumped everything else.

"I'm here because I want to be," he said, then tipped his head to one side and stared at her. "I'm not dropping in to get a look at her before I disappear. Yes, I have an important product launch coming up and I'll have to return to Texas, but I plan on being a permanent part of Caroline's life, which you don't seem to understand. It's interesting to me, though, that suddenly I'm the one defending myself when it's *you* who has all the explaining to do."

"I didn't mean that as an attack on your motives,"

she said quietly. "I just want to make sure you understand exactly what's going to happen here. Once Caroline gives her heart, it's gone forever. You'll hold it and you could crush it without meaning to."

"You're still assuming I'm just passing through."

"No, I'm not." She laughed shortly, but it was a painful sound. "I know you well enough to know that arguing with you is like trying to talk a wall into falling down on its own. Pointless."

He nodded, though the analogy, correct or not, bothered him more than a little. Was he really so implacable all the damn time? "Then we understand each other."

"We do."

"So," he said, with another sip of coffee he really didn't want. "Tell me."

"I'm not sure where to start."

"How about the beginning?" Wes set the coffee down and folded his arms across his chest as he leaned back in his chair. "If you have family money, why the hell did you come to work for me?"

"Rich people can't have jobs?" Offended, she narrowed her eyes on him. "You have money, but you go into the office four days a week. Even when you're at home in Royal, you spend most of your free time on the phone with PR or marketing or whatever. That's okay?"

He squirmed a little in his chair. Maybe she had a point, but he wouldn't concede that easily. "It's my company."

She shook her head. "That's not the only reason.

You're rich. You could hire someone to run the company and you know it. But you *enjoy* your job. Well, so did I."

Hard to argue with the truth. "Okay, I give you that."

"Thank you so much," she muttered.

"But why did you lie to get the job? Why use a fake name?" He cupped his hands around the steaming mug of coffee and watched her.

"Because I wanted to make it on my own." She sighed and sat back, idly spinning the cup in front of her in slow circles. "Being a Graystone always meant that I had roads paved for me. My parents liked to help my brothers and I along the way until finally, I wanted to get out from under my own name. Prove myself, I guess."

"To who?"

She looked at him. "Me."

He could understand and even admire that, Wes realized. Too many people in her position *enjoyed* using the power of their names to get what they wanted whenever they wanted it. Hell, he saw it all the time in business—even in Royal, where the town's matriarchs ruled on the strength of tradition and their family's legacies. The admiration he felt for her irritated hell out of him, because he didn't *want* to like anything about her.

She'd lied to him for years. Hidden his child from him deliberately. So he preferred to hold onto the anger simmering quietly in the pit of his stomach. Though he was willing to cut her a break on how she'd gotten a job at his company, there was *no* excuse for not telling him she was pregnant.

Holding onto the outrage, he demanded, "When you quit your job and left Texas, you didn't bother to tell me you were pregnant. Why?"

"You know why, Wes," she said, shaking her head slowly. "We had that *what if* conversation a few weeks before I found out. Remember?"

"Vaguely." He seemed to recall that one night she'd talked about the future—what they each wanted. She'd talked about kids. Family.

"You do remember," she said softly, gaze on his face. "We were in bed, talking, and you told me that I shouldn't start getting any idea about there being anything permanent between us."

He scowled as that night and the conversation drifted back into his mind.

"You said you weren't interested in getting married," she said, "had no intention of *ever* being a father, and if that's what I was looking for, I should just leave."

It wasn't easy hearing his own words thrown back at him, especially when they sounded so damn cold. Now that she'd brought it all up again, he remembered lying in the dark, Belle curled against his side, her breath brushing his skin as she wove fantasies he hadn't wanted to hear about.

He scraped one hand across his face but couldn't argue with the past. Couldn't pretend now that he hadn't meant every word of it. But still, she should have said something.

"So you're saying it's my fault you said nothing."

"No, but you can see why I didn't rush to confess my pregnancy to a man who'd already told me he had no interest in being a father." She rubbed the spot between her eyes and sighed a little. "You didn't want a child. I did."

"I didn't want a hypothetical child. You didn't give me a choice about Caroline."

"And here we go," she murmured with a shake of her head, "back on the carousel of never-ending accusations. I say something, you say something and we never really *talk*, so nothing gets settled. Perfect."

She had a point. Rehashing old hurts wasn't going to get him the answers he was most interested in. He wanted to know all about his little girl. "Fine. You want settled? Start talking, I'll listen. Tell me about Caroline. Was she born deaf?"

"No." Taking a sip of coffee, she cradled the mug between her palms. "She had normal hearing until the summer she was two."

Outside, the wind blew snow against the window and it hit the glass with a whispering tap. Wes watched her and saw the play of emotions on her face in the soft glow of the overhead lights. He felt a tightness in his own chest in response as he waited for her to speak.

"We spent a lot of time at the lake that summer, and she eventually got an ear infection." Her fingers continued to turn the mug in front of her. "Apparently, it was a bad one, but she was so good, hardly cried ever, and I didn't know anything was wrong with her until she started running a fever.

"I should have known," she muttered, and he could see just how angry she still was at herself for not realizing her child was sick. "Maybe if I'd taken her to the doctor sooner..." She shook her head again and he felt the sense of helplessness that was wrapped around her like a thick blanket.

Wes felt the same way. The story she told had taken place nearly three years ago. He couldn't change it. Couldn't go back in time to be there to help. All he could do now was listen and not say anything to interrupt the flow of words.

She took a breath and blew it out. "Anyway. Her fever suddenly spiked so high one night, I was terrified. We took her to the emergency room—"

"We?" Was she dating some guy? Some strange man had been there for his child when Wes wasn't?

She lifted her gaze to his. "My brother Chance drove us there, stayed with us. The doctors brought her temperature down, gave her antibiotics, and she seemed fine after."

"What happened?"

She sighed and sat back in her chair, folding her arms across her chest as if comforting herself. "When she healed, she had hearing loss. We didn't even notice at first. If there were hints or signs, we didn't see them. It wasn't until the following summer that I realized she couldn't hear the ice cream truck." She smiled sadly. "Silly way to discover something so elemental about your own child, but oh, she used to light up at the sound of those bells."

She took a breath and sighed a little. "The doctors weren't sure exactly what caused it. Could have been the infection itself, the buildup of water in her ears or the effects of the antibiotics. There was just no way to know for sure."

"Wasn't your fault." He met her gaze squarely.

"What?"

"It sounds to me like you couldn't have done anything differently, so it wasn't your fault."

Horrified, he watched her eyes fill with tears. "Hey, hey."

"Sorry." She laughed a little, wiped her eyes and said, "That was just…unexpected. Thank you."

Wes nodded, relieved to see she wasn't going to burst into tears on him. "Will her hearing get worse?"

"Yes." A single word that hit like a blow to the chest. "It's progressive hearing loss. She can still hear now, and will probably for a few more years thanks to the hearing aids, but eventually…"

"What can we do?"

Her eyebrows lifted. "As much as I appreciate you being kind before, there is no *we*, Wes. I am doing everything I can. She wears hearing aids. She's using sign language to expand her conversational skills, and get familiar with it before she actually has to count on it. And I'm considering a cochlear implant."

"I read about those." He leaned his forearms on the table. He'd been doing a lot of reading over the last several hours. There were dozens of different theories and outlooks, but it seemed to him that the cochlear implants were the way to go. Best for everyone. "They're supposed to be amazing. And she's old enough to get one now."

"Yes, I know she is." Belle looked at him and said, "You know, her doctor and I do discuss all of this. He's given me all of the information I need, but it's not critical to arrange surgery for Caro right this minute. It's something I have to think about. To talk about with Caro herself."

Astonished, he blurted, "She's only four."

"I didn't say she'd be making the decision, only that I owe it to her to at least discuss it with her. She's very smart, and whatever decision I make she'll have to live with." She pushed up from the table and carried her unfinished coffee to the sink to pour out. "I'm not foolish enough to let a little girl decide on her own. But she should have a say in it."

"Seriously?" He stood up, too, and walked over to dump his own coffee. He hadn't really wanted it in the first place. "You want to wait when this could help her now? You want to give a four-year-old a vote in what happens to her medically?" Shaking his head, he reached for his cell phone. "I know the best doctors in Texas. They can give me the name of the top guy in this field. We can have Caro in to see the guy by next week, latest."

She snatched the phone right out of his hand and set it down on the counter. "What do you think you're doing?"

"What you're too cautious to do," he said shortly. "Seeing to it that Caro has the best doctor and the best treatment."

Both hands on her hips, she tipped her head back to glare up into his eyes. "You have known about her existence for two days and you really think you have the right to come in here and start giving orders?"

Those green-blue eyes of hers were flashing with indignation and the kind of protective gleam he'd once seen in the eyes of a mother black bear he'd come across in the woods. He'd known then that it wasn't smart to appear threatening to that bear's cubs. And he realized now that maybe trying to jump in and take over was obviously the wrong move. But how the hell could he be blamed for wanting to do *something* for the kid he hadn't even known he had?

"All right." Wes deliberately kept his voice cool, using the reasonable tone he wielded like a finely honed blade in board meetings. "We can talk about it first—"

"*Very* generous," she said as barely repressed fury seemed to shimmer around her in waves. "You're not listening to me, Wes. You don't have a say here. My daughter's name is Caroline *Graystone*. Not Jackson. I make the decisions where she's concerned."

His temper spiked, but he choked it back down. What the hell good would it do for the two of them to keep butting heads? "Do I really have to get a DNA test done to prove I'm now a part of this?"

Her mouth worked as if she were biting back a sharp comeback. And she really looked as if she were trying to find a way to cut him out of the whole thing. But after a few seconds, she took a breath and said, "No. Not necessary."

"Good." Something occurred to him then. "Am I named as her father on the birth certificate?"

"Yes, of course you are." She rinsed out her coffee cup, then turned the water off again. "I want Caro to know who you are—I'd just rather have been the one to pick the time she found out."

"Yeah, well." He leaned against the counter. At least the instant burst of anger had drained away as quickly as it came. "Neither of us got a vote on that one."

The problem of Maverick rose up in his mind again, and he made a mental note to call home again. Find out how the search for the mystery man was going. And it seriously bugged him that he had no idea who it might be. Briefly, he even wondered again if Cecelia and her friends were behind it, in spite of Cecelia's claim of innocence. But for now, he had other things to think about.

"Why does anyone care if you have a child or not? Why is this trending on Twitter?" She sounded as exasperated as he felt, and somehow that eased some of the tension inside him.

"Hell if I know," he muttered and shoved one hand though his hair. "But we live in a celebrity culture now. People are more interested in what some rock star had for dinner than who their damn congressman is."

She laughed a little, surprising him. "I missed that. Who knew?"

"Missed what?" Wes watched the slightest curve of her mouth, and it tugged at something inside him.

"Those mini rants of yours. They last like ten seconds, then you're done and you've moved on. Of course, people around you are shell-shocked for a lot longer…"

"I don't rant." He prided himself on being calm and controlled in nearly all aspects of his life.

"Yeah, you do," she said. "I've seen a few really spectacular ones. But in your defense, you don't do it often."

He frowned as his mind tripped back, looking for other instances of what she called rants. And surprisingly enough, he found a couple. His frown deepened.

"You've got your answers, Wes," she said quietly. "What else do you want here?"

"Some answers," he corrected. "As for what I want, I've already told you. I can't just walk away from my own kid."

"And what do you expect from fatherhood? Specifically."

"I don't know," he admitted. "I just know I have to be here. Have to be a part of her life."

She looked into his eyes for a long second or two before nodding. "Okay. We'll try this. But you have to dial it back a little, too. You're the one trying to fit yourself into *our* lives—not the other way around."

He hated that she had a point. Hated more that as

confident as he was in every damn thing, he had no clue how to get to know a kid. And he *really* didn't like the fact that he was standing this close to Belle and could be moved just by her scent—vanilla, which made him think of cozying up in front of the fire with her on his lap and his hands on her—damn it, this was *not* the way he wanted this to go.

"If you can't agree to that," she said, when he was silent for too long, "then you'll just have to go, Wes."

Fighting his way past his hormones, Wes narrowed his eyes, took a step closer and was silently pleased when she backed up so fast she hit the granite counter. Bracing one hand on either side of her on that cold, black surface, he leaned in, enjoying the fact that he'd effectively caged her, giving her no room to evade him.

"No," he said, his gaze fixed with hers. "You don't want to take orders from me? Well, I sure as hell don't take them from you. I'll stay as long as I want to, and there's not a damn thing you can do about it."

She took a breath, and something flashed in her eyes. Anger, he was guessing, and could only think *join the club*. But it wasn't temper alone sparking in her eyes—there was something more. Something that held far more heat than anger.

"You lied to me for years, Belle. Now I know the truth and until I'm satisfied, until I have everything I want out of this situation, I'm sticking."

She planted both hands flat on his chest and pushed. He let her move him back a step.

"And what is it you want, Wes? What do you expect to find here?"

"Whatever I need."

Four

Whatever I need.

Wes's words echoed in her mind all night long. Even when she finally fell asleep, he was there, in her dreams, taunting her. It was as if the last five years had disappeared. All of the old feelings she'd had for him and had tried so desperately to bury had come rushing back at her the moment she saw him again.

She had three older brothers, so she was used to dealing with overbearing men and knew how to handle them. Isabelle wasn't easily intimidated, and she wasn't afraid to show her own temper or to stand up for herself, either. But what she wasn't prepared for was the rush of desire she felt just being around Wes again.

He was the same force of nature she remembered

him being, and when his focus was directed solely at her, he wasn't an easy man to ignore. Old feelings stirred inside her even though she didn't want them and the only thing that was keeping her sane at the moment was the fact that it wasn't just her own heart in danger, it was Caroline's. And that Isabelle just couldn't risk. She had to find a way to appease Wes, avoid acting on what she was feeling for him and protect Caroline at the same time. She just didn't know yet how she would pull it off.

"Well," Edna said when Isabelle walked into the kitchen. "You look terrible."

Isabelle sighed. Makeup, it seemed, couldn't perform the miracles all the TV commercials promised. "Thanks. Just what I needed to hear."

Edna was in her sixties, with short silver hair that stood up in tufted spikes. Her brown eyes were warm and kind and a little too knowing sometimes. Today she wore her favored black jeans, black sneakers and a red sweatshirt that proclaimed, *For Most of History, Anonymous Was a Woman.—Virginia Woolf.*

"Seriously, did you get *any* sleep?" Edna pulled a mug from under the single-serve coffeemaker and handed it over.

It was gray and cold outside, typical January weather in Colorado. But the kitchen was bright and warm and filled with the scents of coffee and the breakfast Edna insisted on making fresh every morning.

Grateful for the ready coffee, Isabelle took the cup and had her first glorious sip. As the hot caffeine slid into her system, she looked at her housekeeper and gave her a wry smile. "Not much."

Sipping her own coffee, Edna gave her a hard look. "Because of Wes?"

She jolted and stared at the other woman. "How do you know about him?"

"Caro told us this morning. She says he's pretty and that you said he's a friend." Edna tipped her head to one side. "Marco told me to butt out, but who listens to husbands? So, Wes is more than a friend, isn't he?"

Before answering that question, Isabelle looked around and then asked, "Where's Caro?"

"Outside with Marco. She wanted to make sure the snowman they made last weekend was still standing." She paused. "So? Who is he?"

"We've known each other way too long."

Edna laughed. "That's what happens when you grow up in a town of twelve hundred people. We all know too much about each other. Probably keeps us all on the up and up. Can't do a damn thing wrong around here and get away with it." She narrowed her eyes. "And you're stalling."

"I know." Pulling out a stool at the island counter, Isabelle dropped onto it and reached out to grab a biscuit she knew would be stuffed with ham and scrambled eggs. It was Caroline's favorite breakfast, so naturally the indulgent Edna made them a lot. Taking a bite she chewed and said, "He's Caro's father."

"Whoa." Edna's eyebrows shot up. "Wasn't expecting that." She leaned on the countertop. "What does he want?"

"Caro." She took another bite and chewed glumly.

The other woman straightened up in a blink. "Well, he can't have her."

It was good to have friends, Isabelle told herself with a quiet sigh. She'd known Edna and Marco her whole life. They'd both worked for her family since Isabelle was a child. And at an age when they could have retired, instead, they'd come to work for Isabelle, to help raise Caro. And she knew that she would never be able to pay them back for their friendship or their loyalty.

Smiling, Isabelle said, "No, he can't. But to be fair, he doesn't want to take her away, he just wants to be a part of her life."

"That's a bad thing?" Edna pushed the plate of biscuits closer to Isabelle. "Talk and eat. You're too thin."

Isabelle knew it was useless to argue, so she dutifully took another one. "It's not bad necessarily," she said, breaking off a piece of biscuit and egg to pop into her mouth. "But it's…complicated. Caro doesn't know who he is and I don't know how much he's going to push for. Plus, he's so angry that I never told him about her that he's not even trying to be reasonable…"

"Are you?"

Isabelle's gaze shot to Edna's. "Hey. Whose side are you on, anyway?"

"Yours. Absolutely." Reaching over for a dishcloth, Edna wiped up a few crumbs. "But come on, sweetie. The man's a father and you never told him. Most men like to know if their sperm scores a goal."

She snorted a laugh even while she nodded. "True. But he said he didn't want kids."

"That's before he had one." Edna sighed and leaned on the counter again so she could look directly into Isabelle's eyes. "Even Marco didn't want kids till we had our first one."

"That's hard to believe." Frowning, Isabelle remembered how Marco had devoted himself to Edna and their three kids. Even now, he spent most of his free time with their grandchildren. A more family-based man she'd never known.

"Well, it's true." Edna shook her head and grinned. "When I told him I was pregnant the first time, the man went pale—and with that Italian olive complexion of his, it wasn't easy."

Isabelle laughed a little. True.

"My point is, he completely freaked," Edna admitted. "I think he was scared, though God knows a man will never admit to *that*. But once he came around to the idea of being somebody's daddy, he was all for it, and the man is the best father in the world."

"He is," Isabelle murmured.

"So why not cut this Wes guy a break and see what happens?" Edna shrugged. "You two might find a way to work through this."

"Anything's possible, I suppose." But at the moment, Isabelle was having a hard time believing that. She could remember, so clearly, how it had felt to have him looming close to her last night. She'd felt the heat of him reaching for her. And when she'd pushed him away, she'd come very close to grabbing him instead and pulling him closer.

Really irritating that she could be furious with him and *still* want him so badly.

"Is there more going on here than just worry for Caro?" Edna asked quietly.

Isabelle looked at the other woman. "Too much and not enough all at the same time."

Edna took a sip of coffee. "I hate when that happens."

Room service brought him coffee and toast. Wes ate and drank while he ran through the latest stream of emails clogging up his inbox. Deleting as he went, he kept expecting to see another message from Maverick. Why, he didn't know. The damage had already been done. But wouldn't he want to gloat? Wes really hoped so, because just one more email from the mystery man might be enough to help Wes's IT department nail the bastard.

Until that happy day, Wes focused on what he *could* do. The TV was on, the local news channel a constant murmur of sound in the room. One part of Wes's mind paid attention to the reporters, wondering if he'd hear more about this Maverick mess. Meanwhile, he concentrated on answering business emails, then made a call to his VP. When Harry answered, Wes smiled. Good to know his employees were up and working as early as he was.

"Morning, Wes," Harry said. "Sorry to say, if you're calling for an update on Maverick, I don't have one for you yet."

Scowling, Wes rubbed his forehead and walked to the French doors of his suite. It was too damned cold to throw them open, so he settled for holding back the drapes and staring out at Swan Hollow as the small town woke up. The clouds were low and gray—no surprise, and yet more snow was forecasted for today.

"How is it no one can nail this guy—or woman?" Wes grumbled, not really expecting an answer. "Is Maverick some kind of technical ninja or something?"

Harry laughed shortly. "No. So far, he's just been lucky. He got in and out of your account so fast, the IT guys couldn't track him. But Jones in IT tells me he's rigged it to let him know if anyone tries to breach again."

"Well, that's something." It was a lot, really, just not enough. Wes didn't function well with helplessness. Because he'd never accepted it before. Always, he'd been able to do *something*. He'd never been in the position of standing on the sidelines, watching other players make moves he couldn't.

And he didn't like it.

"Not enough, I know," Harry said, as if he knew exactly what Wes was thinking. "But we're still working it. On the downside, Teddy Bradford won't take my call, so if you want to try to do CPR on that merger, you'll have to reach out to him yourself."

"Yeah, I tried before I left Texas. He blew me off, too."

"It may just be over, boss."

"No, I won't accept that," Wes said. "We spent nearly two years putting that merger on the table and I'll be damned before I let some cowardly rumor-monger ruin it. There's a way to save us taking over PlayCo, and I'll find it."

"If you say so," Harry told him, but disbelief was clear in his tone.

Fine, he'd proved people wrong before, and he could do it again. Turning away from the view, Wes voiced a suspicion that had occurred to him only late last night. "You think maybe Teddy's working this from both angles?"

A pause while Harry thought about it. "What exactly do you mean?"

Wes had been turning this over in his mind for hours now, and though it sounded twisted, he thought it could just be true. "Well, we had a deal and he's backed out—what if he and Maverick were in on it together?"

"For what reason?" Harry asked, not shooting down the theory right away.

Any number of reasons, really, Wes told himself, but the most likely one had slipped into his mind last night and refused to leave. "Maybe he's lined up a deal with a different toy company and needed a way to get out of our merger without looking bad."

There was a long pause as Harry considered the idea. "Anything's possible," he said, his voice slow and thoughtful. "I'll put some feelers out. I've got some friends over at Toy America. I'll talk to them. See what I can find out."

"Good. Let me know ASAP if you discover anything." Wes picked up the coffee carafe from the dining table and poured himself another cup. If Bradford was working with Maverick to try to ruin Wes and his company's reputation, heads were going to roll. "I'm going to be here at least a few more days—"

"Yeah." Harry sighed. "Okay, I promised myself I wouldn't ask why you were in Duck Springs, Colorado..."

Unexpectedly, Wes laughed. "Swan Hollow."

"What's the difference?" Harry asked. Then before Wes could speak, he said, "Just tell me. Is everything all right?"

Wes's smile faded slowly. Things were as far from all right as they could get, he thought, but he didn't bother to say anything. Harry and the rest of the company had probably figured out that Maverick's email about Wes's daughter had been nothing but the truth. But that didn't mean he was ready to discuss it with everyone. Not even his friend Harry.

"Yeah," he said, gulping coffee. "Everything's fine. I just have a few...personal issues to work out."

Understatement of the century. There was so much rushing through his mind, he hadn't gotten more than a couple of hours of sleep all night. And this morning, Wes felt like his eyeballs had been rolled around in sand. In those long sleepless hours, his brain had raced with images, ideas. A daughter. The dead merger. A saboteur—perhaps even his ex—trying to take down his business. And then there was Belle. A woman he should know better than to want—yet apparently his body hadn't gotten that memo.

"If you say so." Harry didn't sound convinced, but then he added, "When you're ready to talk about it, I'm here. And if I can do something, let me know."

"Find Maverick," Wes said. "That's what I need you to do. Keep everyone on it. I want to know who and where this guy is."

"We're working it, boss. Do what you have to do and don't worry about what's going on back in Houston. We'll find him. I'll be in touch."

After Harry hung up, Wes tossed his phone onto the couch and grabbed the remote when he saw the stock report flash onto the television screen. Draining his coffee cup, he punched up the volume and then cursed as the anchor started speaking.

"Things are not looking good for TTG Inc.," the man said in a low, deep voice. "Texas Toy Goods' stock has taken a hard dip over the last couple of days. CEO Wes Jackson has not yet commented on the short-lived scandal that apparently was behind Teddy Bradford of PlayCo announcing the end of their much-anticipated merger."

The stocks reporter then turned to the digital screen behind him and tracked the TTG stock on a downward slide. Meanwhile Wes's temper inched up in an opposite trajectory.

"TTG Inc.," the man said, "is down five points,

and my sources say there are no immediate plans to put the merger back in play. PlayCo, the anticipated merger partner, on the other hand, has ticked up two points in the last twenty-four hours."

Disgusted, Wes hit the mute button and wished fervently that his thoughts were as easy to silence. One thing he knew for sure. Once a stock started slipping, the whole thing took on a life of its own. People would worry and sell off their stock and his price would dip even lower.

He had to put a stop to this before he lost everything he'd worked for. Stalking to the carafe of coffee, he refilled his cup and carried it with him to the door when a knock sounded.

Who the hell could that be? Room service had already come and gone. He doubted very much that Belle would be dropping in for a visit. And he was in no mood to talk to anybody else. Riding on temper, he yanked the door open and demanded, "What?"

A tall man in a heavy brown coat with a sheepskin collar stood on the threshold. He had narrowed blue eyes, short, light brown hair and a neatly trimmed beard. Two men with a slight resemblance to the first man stood right behind him, and not one of them looked happy to be there. Wes braced himself for whatever was coming.

"You Wes Jackson?" The first man spoke while the other two continued to glare at Wes.

"Yeah, I am." He met that flat cool stare with one of his own. "Who're you?"

"Chance Graystone."

Damn it. Well, Belle had warned him about her older brothers. Looked like he was going to meet the family whether he wanted to or not.

Chance jerked a thumb over his shoulder. "My brothers, Eli and Tyler. We're here to talk to you."

"That's great." They didn't give Wes an opportunity to shut the door on them. Instead, all three of them pushed past him into the room. Each of them somehow managing to give Wes an accidental shove as they did.

"Well, sure," he said. "Come on in."

All three men stood in the living room of the suite, waiting for him. Their stances were identical. Feet braced wide apart, arms across their chests, features cold, mouths tight. They could have stepped right out of an old Western movie—three sheriffs ready to face the outlaw. Who would, he told himself, be *him*.

There was no avoiding this. Slowly, Wes closed the door then glanced down into the cup he held. "This is not gonna be enough coffee."

Still, he took a sip to steel himself then deliberately took his time as he strolled out to meet Belle's brothers. He had no idea what was coming. Did they want to talk? Fight? Ride him out of town on a rail? Who the hell knew? Setting his coffee cup down on the closest table, he faced the three men. Wes guessed Chance was the oldest, since he took the lead in the conversation.

"We're here to set you straight on a few things."

"Is that right?" Wes wasn't intimidated, though he had the feeling the Graystone brothers were used to putting the fear of God into whoever happened to be standing against them at the time. Well, they were going to have a hard time with him. He didn't scare easily, and he *never* backed down when he knew he was right.

"That's about it," Chance said in a flat, dark voice. "Isabelle's our sister. Caro's our niece. You do anything to hurt either one of them and we're going to have a problem."

Wes shifted his stance to mock the three men facing him. Arms across his chest, he glared at each of them in turn before settling his gaze back on Chance. "I'd say that what happens between Belle and me is our business."

Chance took a single step forward. "Then you'd be wrong. You made your choice. You let her walk out of your life five years ago."

Though he might have a point, Wes didn't acknowledge it. "She didn't tell me about our daughter."

The two brothers behind Chance exchanged a quick look. "He's right about that," one of them said.

Chance nodded. "Yeah, she should have told you. I give you that."

"Thanks," Wes said wryly.

"We told her so when she first came home. It wasn't right, her keeping it from you."

"Agreed."

"But Isabelle does things her way. Always has. She doesn't take advice well."

"Yeah," Wes said. "Me neither. Who knew she and

I would have that in common?" One of the brothers—Eli or Tyler, he didn't know which was which—smiled at that. "Just how did you guys know I was here? Did Belle send you to scare me off?"

"This is a small town, man. Word started spreading the minute you drove up to Isabelle's house, and the talk hasn't slowed down since." Chance laughed shortly. "Besides, there is no way Isabelle would have come running to us. Our little sister doesn't need a man to protect her."

Wes waved one hand at the three of them. "And yet..."

Chance smiled slightly. "Just because she doesn't need it doesn't mean she won't get it."

He could understand that. Family standing for family. But knowing that didn't mean he liked being warned off or threatened.

"Fine." Wes nodded and met Chance's steady gaze with his own. "I'm not here to hurt Belle. I'm here to connect with my daughter. And," he added, "there's no way you can stop me."

A long, tension-filled silence followed as the men took each other's measure. Wes didn't flinch. He'd faced down adversaries before. He'd been in his share of fistfights growing up, and he'd won them all. He'd looked across boardroom tables at competitors aching to take him down, and he hadn't folded to anyone. Damned if he'd start now. A part of him admired Belle's brothers. Loyalty was everything to him, and maybe that's why Belle's lies had cut so deeply. But he could understand these men standing up for their sister even as he knew it wouldn't stop him from doing what he'd come to Swan Hollow to do.

Finally, Chance nodded. "Can't say that I blame you for coming here. Actually, under other circumstances, I might even like you for it."

Wes laughed.

"But we'll be watching," Chance promised. "You make Isabelle or Caroline unhappy—it won't be pretty."

"Seems fair," Wes agreed. "As long as you three understand I'll be staying in town as long as I please. I'll see my daughter and your sister as often as I can manage it, and I don't want any of you interfering. This is between Belle and I."

Chance's gaze locked with Wes's for a long moment. Then he nodded. "I think we have an understanding."

"And you're not going to have an easy time of it," one of the other brothers quipped, a half smile on his face. "Isabelle's got a head like a rock when her mind's made up. And she's probably not real happy that you're here."

Wes frowned, and Chance laughed at his expression.

"Yeah," the man said a second later. "I'm thinking Tyler's right and you've got bigger problems with Isabelle than you do dealing with us."

Belle's brothers silently filed out of the room. Wes stayed where he was and didn't watch them go.

He'd been alone since his father's death a few

years earlier. No siblings, no extended family, and since he'd never known anything different, he hadn't really missed it, either. Until just now. But even he could see that the Graystone siblings were tight. Close-knit. And a part of him he hadn't even been aware of was almost jealous of it.

Then his mind started clicking. Thoughts, ideas, possible plans flashed through his brain so quickly he couldn't separate them all. But somewhere in the chaos of his thoughts there was a single notion that began to shine brightly. If he could make it work, it might solve everything.

Yes, he wanted Maverick caught. Dealt with. The man—or whoever—had cost him a merger Wes had spent two years setting up. On the other hand, if not for Maverick, he might never have known about his daughter's existence. Wes didn't want another relationship with Belle—she'd lied to him for five years. But he did want to be a part of Caroline's life.

And as his mind worked, he realized there might be a way to salvage that merger after all. As long as he was here, in Colorado, spending time with Caro and Belle anyway, he might be able to use this time to convince the CEO of PlayCo that he, Belle and Caroline were a happy little family. Teddy Bradford wanted family values? Well, Wes might be in a position to offer that. *If* Bradford wasn't behind the Maverick mess himself.

It was a thought. Something to look at, maybe plan for. Making the best of a situation was what

Wes did. And that damn merger meant too much to just walk away from it.

The key to all of this came down to one word. A word Wes had avoided for years, but now it had caught him, held him and wouldn't let go.

Family.

Five

An hour later, after leaving Caro in her pre-K classroom, Belle found Wes waiting for her in the parking lot. He was leaning against a huge black SUV, watching her, and he looked…dangerous. Okay, maybe that was just her. The day was bright and freezing, with high clouds studding a deep blue sky. Pine trees were layered with snow, and high barriers of the white stuff lined the parking lot where it had been pushed by the maintenance crew.

She'd like to think Wes looked out of place at the school in his black jeans, forest green sweater and black leather jacket. The truth was, he fit in everywhere. His blond hair ruffled in the wind, and as he pulled his sunglasses off to look at her, she noted his eyes were narrowed against the glint of the sun off the snow.

He looked dark, edgy, and her heart gave a hard thump she couldn't deny. Having Wes come back into her life was throwing everything off balance. Thoughts of him had kept her awake all night as her brain replayed memories she'd tried to bury for the past five years.

Working with him had been challenging, but fun. As focused as he was on his own vision, Wes had always been the kind of boss to welcome other ideas besides his own. That made for a great working environment, and Isabelle had loved being a part of it—until she fell in love with the boss. Then, everything had changed for her.

She'd let herself believe that the partnership she felt with him at work could extend to the personal, too. But even when they were alone together, at their most intimate, Isabelle had felt Wes pulling back. And the harder she tried to reach him, the more elusive he became. Finally, she'd had to realize that he wouldn't change. Would never be able to love her as she loved him and that waiting and hoping would slowly wear her heart away like waves against rock, until there was nothing left.

Now, he was back. Pushing himself into her life whether she liked it or not. Refusing to go away. It seemed, she thought, that Wes would always do the opposite of what she wanted him to.

All around her, the sidewalk and parking lot was alive with people. Parents soothing toddlers, folks starting cars, rushing off to the rest of their days. But all she could see was Wes.

She headed toward him. "What are you doing here?"

"Wanted to see her school." He pushed away from what was probably a rental. "Wanted to see you."

Just five years ago, those words would have turned her heart inside out. Now, she was worried. Why did he want to see her? Before she could find out, someone called her name.

"Isabelle!" She turned and smiled tightly at the woman hurrying toward her.

"Hi, Kim. What's up?" From the corner of her eye, Isabelle saw Wes approaching. Kim's reaction was instantaneous and completely predictable. The woman's eyes widened in appreciation, and a soft, speculative curve lifted her mouth.

Typical.

"What can I do for you?" Isabelle asked, drawing the woman's attention back to her.

"Oh. Right." She smiled at Wes again as he walked up to stand beside Isabelle. "Sorry. I just wanted to remind you that you volunteered to provide refreshments for the girls' dance recital next week."

"Sure. Thanks for the reminder," Isabelle said, "I've been so...busy, I'd forgotten."

"I don't blame you for being...*busy*," Kim said, shifting her gaze to Wes again. "Hello. I'm Kim Roberts."

He took her hand in his. "Wes Jackson."

She never took her eyes from his as she said, "Isabelle, you've been keeping this gorgeous man all to yourself? Selfish."

Kim was doing everything but drooling, and Isabelle had to squelch a flash of irritation. Just like the old days, she told herself. Even when Isabelle was standing right beside him, women would coo and practically purr at him, completely ignoring Isabelle's presence.

"Wes is an old…friend of mine from Texas," she said and scowled when he smiled at her explanation. "He's here visiting."

"Well," Kim said, her smile brightening enough that she looked like an actress in a toothpaste commercial, "maybe we could get together while you're in town. I'd love to show you around."

"Thanks," Wes said, "but I think Isabelle's got that covered." He turned his back on Kim and asked Isabelle, "Are you ready to go?"

"What? Oh. Yes." Surprised that he had turned down Kim's oh-so-generous offer, Isabelle looked up at him and wondered, not for the first time, what he was thinking. He tugged at her arm and she'd actually started walking with him until she realized he was escorting her to his car. Then she stopped. "My car's here."

"We'll come back for it later." He helped her into the oversize Suburban, then closed the door.

Kim was staring after them, a look of shock on her features. It had probably been years since a man had shown such a lack of interest in her. Sadly, Isabelle knew that Kim would only react to his response as a challenge. She liked Kim, but the woman was always on the prowl for her next ex-husband.

"She's interested in you, you know," Isabelle said as Wes drove through the parking lot and out onto the street.

He snorted. "That type's interested in everything male."

"That was rude," Isabelle muttered. "True, but rude. Anyway, where are we going?"

"I don't know," he said, aiming the car for Main Street. "Why don't you tell me? What do you usually do after dropping Caroline at school?"

Frowning, she half turned in her seat to look at him. Even his profile looked hard, implacable. Why was it she liked that about him even as it drove her crazy? Okay, fine, he was here to see Caroline. But why was he spending time with *her*? "What's this about, Wes? Do you plan to just follow me around town?"

He shrugged. "Would you rather we go back to your place and talk?"

"No." Being alone with him wasn't a good idea. Even knowing better, she might be tempted to—nope.

"There you go. So where are we headed?"

She sighed. The man was nothing if not determined. Rather than argue with him, she surrendered. "Business supply store," she said. "I need a new laser printer and some other supplies."

One eyebrow winged up. "Still working? What do you do now?"

"What I always did. I design toys, only now I freelance," she said, turning her face to look out the window at Swan Hollow as it flashed past.

"For who?"

She thought about not telling him, but the minute she considered it, she let it go. The man could find out the truth easily enough if he did a little digging online. So really, it was pointless to try to keep it a secret even though she didn't love the idea of allowing him even deeper into her life.

"Myself," she said, keeping her gaze focused out the side window so she didn't have to look at him.

"Right," he said wryly, "because rich people can work, too."

She whipped her head around to glare at him. "Why is it when *you* have your own company that's okay, but when I do, I'm a rich dilettante just killing time?"

"I didn't say that."

"You didn't have to." She took a breath and let it out again. "Besides, my life is not your business."

"If that life concerns Caro, then you're wrong. It is."

"Where is this coming from?" She squirmed in her seat and wished she were on her feet so she could pace off the nervous energy pulsing inside her. "You never wanted kids, so why are you so fixated on involving yourself with Caro?"

"Because she's *mine*," he said and stepped on the

brake for a red light. Turning to meet her eyes, he said, "I protect what's *mine*."

"So it's just a pride thing?" she asked, trying to read his features, his eyes, hoping she'd see something that would reassure her. That would let her know they'd find a way to work all this out. But as usual, Wes hid what he was thinking, feeling, locking it all down behind an impenetrable wall.

"You hid my daughter from me, Belle. That's not a pride thing, that's a damn fact."

His eyes flashed, a muscle in his jaw flexed and his hands fisted on the steering wheel. Staring into those intense eyes of his, Isabelle knew that he would be a formidable enemy. But was that really what they'd come to? Were they so obviously on opposite sides of this one issue that there would be no way to reach some kind of accord?

He couldn't use his money against her, because she had plenty of her own. But she couldn't use hers against him for the same reason—there, at least, they were on equal ground.

But what would a court say, she suddenly wondered. If he got a lawyer and sued for custody, would the judge punish her for keeping Caroline from him for years? Would he order her daughter turned over to her father? A way to make up to him for all the time he'd lost with Caro? God, that thought opened up a hole inside her.

"I did what I thought was the best thing for me," she said softly. "For Caroline."

"Well," he snapped as the light turned green and he stepped on the gas again, "you were wrong."

But she hadn't been wrong at all, Belle thought. The only thing she'd done wrong was get caught.

"Your brothers came to see me this morning."

"They what?" The change in subject was so startling, it completely threw her off. But a second later, Isabelle gritted her teeth and rolled her eyes. This was her own fault. She had planned to tell her brothers today about Wes being in town. She should have known that they would hear the town grapevine buzzing long before that. Rubbing her fingers against her forehead, trying to fight a headache that seemed to have settled in permanently, Isabelle reminded herself that Chance, Eli and Tyler loved her. They were just being protective. They were looking out for Caroline.

Nope, trying to calm herself down wasn't working, she thought. She was still furious. "What did they do?"

One corner of his mouth quirked in response to the tone of her voice.

"You think this is amusing?" she asked, stunned at the sudden shift in his attitude.

"I didn't this morning," he admitted. "When they pushed their way into my hotel room, my first instinct was to go a few rounds with them. But now, seeing how them interfering really frosts you, yeah. It's amusing."

"That's great," she said, nodding as her world tipped even farther off balance. "You're bonding with my brothers. I should have expected that. You're all so much alike."

"Excuse me?"

She glanced at him. "Now you're offended. That's what I find funny." Shaking her head, she said, "You don't even see it. You, Chance, Eli and Tyler are all pushy, domineering, know-it-alls. You think you know what's best for *everyone* and none of you are willing to listen to reason."

"Reason?" he repeated. "I think I've been pretty damn reasonable so far."

"Ah," she said, lifting one hand. "*So far* being the key words in that sentence. How do I know you're not going to suddenly decide to sue me for custody of Caro?" she asked, blurting out her deepest fear. "How do I know you're not already planning to take her away from me?"

"Because I just found out about her two days ago?" he asked. "I'm good, but even I need more time than that."

He parked the car in the lot and shut off the engine, and Isabelle shifted in her seat to look at him. "How much time, Wes? How long do I have before you come after me with all of your lawyers?"

Wes shifted in his seat, too, until they faced each other in the closed-off silence of the big car. Outside, people wandered in and out of the store and a few more clouds filled the sky, threatening more of the snow that still covered the parking lot. "Who said anything about lawyers?"

"I've been waiting for *you* to say it," she admitted. "But just know, if you bring lawyers into it, so will I."

"Yeah, I know." He nodded grimly. "So no lawyers. We do this between us."

Isabelle released a breath she hadn't realized she'd been holding. For now, at least, she didn't have to worry about Wes taking her to court. He might change his mind later, but she'd be grateful for today. "Okay, good. So how do we settle this?"

"To start? You get used to me being here. Being with Caroline. I'll jet back and forth to Texas as needed for business, but I plan on being here. A lot. Don't fight me on it, Belle," he warned. "We'll figure the rest out as we go."

She didn't like it. But why would she? Still, she liked this better than the idea of a protracted courtroom drama where they ended up at each other's throats. That wouldn't be good for Caro—or for any of them. It went against every instinct she had to let him into her and her daughter's lives. But the way she saw it, she just didn't have a choice.

Staring into those beautiful eyes of his, she felt that near magnetic pull that she'd always experienced around him. That was dangerous, but only to her. Isabelle knew she would have to be on guard—and never let him know what he could do to her with just a look. Her reawakened feelings aside, it would be easier all the way around if she could just get through this situation with Wes without slipping back into dangerous feelings.

Wes hadn't wanted a family—kids. Finding out

that she had kept Caroline from him had hit him in his pride, so naturally he'd had to come here. Had to get answers. But it wouldn't last, she told herself. He'd spend some time here and then he'd go back to his real life and she could return to normal. All she had to do was hang on until Wes remembered that he liked being unencumbered by a family.

"So are we good?" he demanded.

He was watching her, waiting.

"Yes," she said. "We're good. For now." And that was the best she could give him.

"That's a start," he said and opened the car door.

Much later, bedtime was a little crazier than usual. Caroline was fascinated with Wes, and Isabelle couldn't blame her. When Wes smiled, the female heart melted. Didn't matter if you were four or eighty-four, the man had a power. For the last five years, Isabelle had assured herself that she was immune to Wes's charms.

It was a hard thing to discover that she'd been lying to herself, too.

"Another story!" Caroline said, grinning up at Wes. The two of them were sitting on the floor in front of her bed.

Isabelle leaned one shoulder against the doorjamb and folded her arms across her chest. She couldn't tear her eyes off the man and his daughter. Just like she couldn't help wondering where they would all be right now if she had told Wes about Caroline from the beginning. Would he have changed? Would he have wanted the three of them to be a family?

Had she cheated all of them out of what they might have had? God, that was a terrible thought and one that couldn't do the slightest bit of good. What she had to do now was concentrate on the moment at hand and not get lost in memories or dreams of *what if.*

Wes had a book on his lap, and while he read the story out loud, he also tried to use sign language. The movements were a little clumsy, and he got quite a few of the hand signs completely wrong. Isabelle noticed Caroline giggling a little when Wes read the word *bear* and signed something entirely different. But making mistakes wasn't important. The fact that he was trying, that he was going to the trouble to learn ASL tugged at Isabelle's heart.

"Wes," Caro said and signed, "read the one about Christmas."

He feigned dramatic shock. "Christmas is over."

"Not *next* Christmas," Caro argued, with a little giggle that rippled through Isabelle's heart.

"Three stories is enough, Caroline," Isabelle said from the doorway, and the girl and her father both turned to look at her. Two sets of eyes the color of the sea in the Caribbean studied her. She saw Wes in her daughter every day, but seeing the two of them together like this, the resemblance was heartbreaking.

She wasn't blind here. Not only was Wes enjoying this time with Caroline, but her little girl already adored him. Once she found out Wes was her father, that affection would be sealed forever. And again, Isabelle felt that twinge of guilt for keeping them apart.

"Mommy…" Caro dipped her head, looked up and let her bottom lip jut out just enough for a really good pout.

Isabelle laughed in spite of herself. "Not a chance, kiddo. Now get into bed and I'll tuck you in."

Dragging herself to her feet, Caro sighed heavily, turned and crawled under the covers, tugging them up to her chin. "Can Wes tuck me in tonight?"

Wow. Arrow to her heart. Shifting a glance to Wes, she saw the pleasure shining in his eyes, and that actually took a bit of the sting out of Caro's request. She'd never had to share her daughter with another parent before. The joys, the worries, the sleepless nights had all been for her alone. But standing in the bedroom with Wes, both of them looking at the child they'd created together, Isabelle could almost see what she'd been missing. It was more than sharing the responsibilities. It was sharing those secret looks of pride and understanding when their child did something cute. Or silly. Or tender.

So Isabelle took a step forward, into that joint custody world. Bending down, she gave Caro a kiss and whispered, "Sleep tight. I love you."

Then she stepped aside and let Wes be the one to smooth the sheet and blanket, to sweep soft, silky hair back off their girl's forehead. He kissed her cheek and said, "Good night, Caroline."

"G'night," she said on a yawn. "Will I see you some more tomorrow?"

Wes straightened up and glanced at Isabelle meaningfully before looking back at his daughter. "You sure will."

For the next week, Isabelle felt like a caged tiger in the zoo. Someone was always watching her—and that someone was Wes. Every time she turned around, there he was. At the grocery store. At Caro's school—where he'd charmed the little girl's teacher until the woman was practically a puddle of goo in front of him.

He showed up at her house nearly every evening, bringing dinner with him—which endeared him to Edna, who enjoyed the time off from cooking. He helped Marco pull a tree stump from the backyard, and now Isabelle had to listen to Marco's glowing remarks about a "city man" who knew how to put in a real day's work.

But the worst, she thought, as she pulled into the school parking lot, was Caro herself. The little girl was completely in love with her father.

Wes had plenty of charm when he wanted to use it, as Belle was in a position to know. But she'd never really stood back and watched as he made a conquest. The women in town, Edna, they were one thing, but seeing Caro respond to her father's determination to win her over had been both touching and worrisome. The harder Caro fell for Wes, the easier it would be for him to eventually break the girl's heart. Though to be honest, she hadn't really seen any sign of Wes pulling away. Instead, he seemed focused on being an integral part of Caro's life.

And all of it worried Isabelle. Sooner or later, he would return to Texas. What then? Would he want to take Caroline back with him? Would they end up in a bitter custody fight after all? Or would he have his fill of playing daddy and just leave—breaking Caroline's heart? Even a best-case scenario was filled with possible misery. Say she and Wes worked it out together and he didn't get tired of being a father? Wouldn't he want Caro with him in Texas for at least part of the year?

Isabelle's head hurt, and she didn't see any relief in her near future. So she pushed all of those thoughts out of her mind and tried instead to focus on her work.

She went over the last of her digital drawings, adding a touch of color here, smoothing a sharp line there, until she was completely satisfied. Well, *completely* was a stretch. She was never truly satisfied with her work, and invariably, once she'd sent the drawings off, she would think of dozens of things she could have done differently.

But the most important thing here was getting her latest designs to the manufacturer who could get started on production. Isabelle sent off a quick email, attaching the designs, and then shifted her attention to the paperwork that had been mounting over the last few days.

"You work from home?"

Isabelle jolted in her chair, glanced at the open doorway to her home office and slapped one hand to her chest when she saw Wes standing there. "How did you get in?"

"Edna let me in. Told me you were up here."

Traitor, Isabelle thought. Her housekeeper was clearly indulging her inner matchmaker. Too bad the woman didn't know that Wes wasn't interested in a match of any kind. Isabelle's heart ached a little at that internal reminder. It would be so much easier for her if she could just get past the feelings for him that kept resurfacing.

He strolled into the room, hands in his pockets, and wandered the perimeter, invading her space, looking at everything. She bit her tongue, because telling him to get out of her office would only make him that much more determined to look around. He took long, slow strides, moving with a sort of stealthy grace that made her insides quiver completely against her will.

Taking a deep breath, Isabelle watched as he checked out the full-color digital printouts of her latest sketches she had taped to a wall and the easel where one of her charcoal sketches was on display. Then he moved onto the dry erase board, with her schedule laid out, and finally to the corkboard where she'd affixed dozens of pictures of children holding toys.

Her office was at the front of the house on the second floor. Caroline called it the tower room. The windows looked out over a landscape that included the woods full of snow-covered pines, a lake, and in the distance, mountains that looked tall enough to scrape the sky.

The room wasn't very big, but she didn't need a massive office since there was no one to impress. She had a desk with a computer, an easel and paints, and space enough to pace when she needed to think. But right now, Isabelle wished for a much bigger space, because her office seemed to have shrunk the moment Wes walked into it.

"What is all this?" he asked quietly, turning at last to look at her.

"My work. It's what I do now," she told him and stood up from behind her desk. She didn't want to be seated while he loomed over her. "I set up a nonprofit that provides toys to hospitalized children. I call it Caro's Toybox."

She didn't look at him, instead focusing on the pictures of the smiling kids she kept in her office as inspiration. "I do the design work and the manufacturer produces the toys, then we distribute them."

He looked at those smiling faces in the photographs, too, and asked, "How'd you get into this?"

Isabelle walked up to stand beside him so that both of them were looking at those happy faces staring back at them. "When Caro was so sick, and then diagnosed, we spent a lot of time in the local hospital. We saw ill, scared children, and I realized that stuffed animals, or dolls, or even a toy plane could bring comfort to those kids when no one was around."

She sighed as memories rushed into her mind—sharing waiting rooms with other worried mothers, hearing the muffled cries of children, punctuated by an occasional wail of pain.

"I held Caro on my lap as doctors poked and prodded her. She was scared, but she had me there to try to comfort her," she said sadly. "But there were a lot of kids on the ward who spent too much time alone in their beds. Their moms and dads had other kids to take care of, and jobs, too. Nurses are amazingly great, but they're frantically busy and can't always take the time to try to ease a child's fear."

"I wish I'd been there. For Caro. For you." His voice was low, soft and tinged with regret.

Isabelle looked at him and saw his features soften and felt closer to him than she ever had. Whether he'd been there or not, he was Caroline's father, and only the two of them could really understand what it was like to have a sick child you couldn't help.

"I wish you had been, too." She looked up at him. "I know it's my fault that you weren't, and for that, I'm really sorry."

He looked down at her, and his clear aqua eyes shone with emotion that he couldn't hide. "Thanks. For saying that. For meaning it."

Isabelle's heart thumped hard in her chest. Her stomach swirled with anticipation, expectation and a jolt of nerves that only increased with every breath she drew. "I do, Wes," she said. "If I could do it all over…"

He shook his head, reached out and laid one hand

on her shoulder. "We can't do any of it over. But we can do it differently from here on."

The heat of his touch drifted down, sliding into her chest and filling her with a kind of warmth she hadn't known in five years. Staring into his eyes, she was drawn in by that magnetic pull she'd always felt around him. It took everything she had to keep from moving into him, wrapping her arms around his neck and kissing him. But that would only make this moment even more confusing than it already was.

So she only reached up to cover his hand with her own. "We can do that."

He released her as his eyes warmed and a half smile curved his mouth. "Good." He shifted his gaze back to the faces on her board. "So you decided to try to take care of all of those kids," he said.

"To do what I could, yes." She too looked at the board where smiling children were caught in a moment of time. "We set up a toy room on the pediatric floor—" She broke off and chuckled. "Nothing fabulous, of course, usually a maintenance closet that we take over. We add shelves, paint and stock it with toys. Then every new patient gets to choose a toy for themselves."

She smiled a little, remembering the excitement of the kids when they were given the chance to go toy shopping right in the hospital. "It's a good feeling, watching children go into the room and inspect everything there before making their choice."

"Yeah," he said softly, "I bet it is."

She felt him looking at her, and she turned her

head to meet his gaze. He was giving her a quizzical look, as if he was trying to figure her out. "What is it?"

He shook his head. "Nothing. I'm just…impressed."

"And surprised?"

"No, not really," he said, tipping his head to one side to look at her more deeply. "You always had a big heart."

Now *she* was the one shocked. And a little off balance. These few moments with Wes had fundamentally changed how they were dealing with each other. Which was good for Caroline, but dangerous for Isabelle. Old feelings were awakened and new ones were jolting into life. "Well, it's getting late, and I need to pick up Caro at school."

"Yeah," he said. "I'll go with you. But first…" He paused, looked down at her and said, "I'd like to help you. With this."

"What?"

"If you had more toys available, you could get into more hospitals, right?" He studied each smiling face on the board as if committing them each to memory.

"Well, yes," she said, watching him. "We've been moving slowly, running on donations and what we can produce. It's taking longer than I'd like."

"Then let me help," he said, and this time he turned to her and reached out to hold her upper arms in a soft, firm grip. "What you're doing is something special. Something important, and it makes me proud that you started it all. So let me in, Belle. Let me be a part of what you do."

Her heart jumped into a fast, heavy rhythm. His eyes on hers, she saw his sincerity. Saw how much he wanted this and what it meant to him. She was touched more deeply than she'd expected. With Wes's help she could grow her program faster than ever before. They could reach more children. Offer more comfort. That he wanted to do this meant more to her than anything else he could have done.

"I'd like that very much," she said.

A slow, satisfied smile curved his mouth, and his eyes gleamed. He rubbed his hands up and down her arms, creating a friction that kindled the heat already building inside her.

"Thanks for that," he said. "I think we'll make a great team."

Isabelle smiled, but her heart hurt a little, since five years ago, she'd thought the same thing.

Six

If anyone had told Wes a month ago that he'd be sitting front row center at a four-year-old's dance recital, he would have called them crazy. Yet, here he was. And most amazing of all, he was having a good time.

Isabelle sat beside him, and next to her were Edna and Marco. On Wes's right, Chance, Eli and Tyler sprawled in the too-small chairs, trying to get comfortable. The elementary school auditorium was packed with parents, grandparents and kids of all ages. The room was big, the chairs were uncomfortable and in the corner beside the stage, an elderly woman was playing a piano that looked as if it could have been one of the first ones ever made.

Smiling to himself, he shook his head and leaned in when Isabelle whispered, "Look over there."

He followed her gaze and spotted Caro, standing in the wings, peeking around the stage curtain. When she saw him, she grinned and her little face brightened. She waved, then made the sign for *thank you*. His heart did a slow, hard roll in his chest as he signed back *you're welcome.*

Of course she didn't have to thank him for coming. There was literally nowhere else he'd rather be than here, waiting to see his little girl take part in a dance recital. With the help of the hearing aids she wore, Caro could hear the music well enough to participate in the dancing she loved. Wes frowned thoughtfully to himself as Caro ducked back behind the curtain to join her class.

How long, he wondered, would the hearing aids work? How long before she entered a completely silent world? He'd been doing research on the cochlear implant, and the more he read the more certain he was that he wanted to get Caroline to a specialist as soon as possible. Yes, he knew that there were many, many happy, healthy deaf people and he knew that Caro would no doubt have a fulfilled life no matter which path she took. But was it so wrong for a father to do everything he could to try to make his child's life a little easier?

He glanced at Isabelle, who had the look of a nervous mom. Her blond hair waved and curled across her shoulders, and as she listened to Edna, she laughed quietly and her greenish-blue eyes shone. She wore a red silk shirt and black slacks, and just looking at her sent a jolt of desire whipping through Wes that he fought like hell to tamp down.

Ever since their talk in her office a couple of days ago, the tension between them had eased in one way and tightened in another. Though there was less anger, more understanding now, the sexual buzz they shared was stronger than ever. Hell, it had been five years since he'd been with her, and sitting beside her now, it was all he could think about.

But he had to move carefully. Slowly. He couldn't give in to what he wanted if his desires were going to make everything else harder. He needed to get his daughter to a specialist. He needed to save the merger, though right now that looked impossible. And soon, he was going to have to be back in Texas to take care of the business he couldn't handle over the phone. And he wanted Belle and Caroline to go with him. Sex would just complicate everything.

Damn it.

"Oh, hell," Chance muttered from beside him. "Hide me."

Frowning, Wes looked up and saw Kim Roberts headed their way, her gaze fixed on the oldest Graystone brother. Wes was so pleased her laser focus was on someone other than *him*, he couldn't even feel sorry for Chance.

"They're starting!" Isabelle reached over, grabbed Wes's hand and squeezed as the piano music got louder and the lights in the hall were dimmed.

"Thank God," Chance mumbled as Kim had to retreat and find a seat. "Saved by tiny dancers."

Wes grinned, then everything in the room faded away but his daughter, one of a dozen little girls dressed as butterflies as they pranced across the stage. Brightly colored tissue paper wings fluttered, pigtails bounced and nervous giggles erupted in more than a few of the performers. In the darkness, he and Isabelle held hands, linked together by one beautiful little girl and the heat threatening to engulf them both.

After the performance, Wes stood apart from the group of parents, siblings and relatives. He was watching them all as his mind raced. His gaze fixed on Belle, behind the refreshment counter, laughing, talking and serving punch, cookies and cupcakes. And he thought he'd never seen anything more beautiful.

Wes wasn't kidding himself. He had no more interest in love than he ever had. But he could admit he wanted Belle. And that he needed her. In more ways than one. If he could convince Teddy Bradford that he, Belle and Caroline were really a happy little family, then he might be able to salvage the merger that meant so much to his company.

If he felt a twinge of something that could have been guilt, he denied it. He wasn't planning to use Belle and Caroline. But it was hardly his fault if being with his daughter and Belle helped solve a major problem.

He wandered toward the table and stepped up in time to listen in as Caro began a step-by-step description of the performance they'd just seen. Words rushing, fingers flying, his little girl was quivering with excitement, and Wes loved every second of it. Seeing his daughter with her blond hair in pigtails, big aqua eyes wide with happiness, made him smile. She was so small that her butterfly wings really did look as if they could lift her into the sky, but it was her tiny pink ballet shoes that for some reason struck his heart like an arrow.

She'd gotten to him, he realized. In little more than a week, Caroline had become so important to him, he couldn't imagine a life without his daughter. He'd never expected, or wanted, to be a parent, and now he couldn't imagine why. He wanted to tell Caroline he was her father. But he wasn't going to do that then disappear back to Texas and only be involved in her life in the most peripheral way.

He wanted more. Wanted to be there every damn day to watch her grow up. To be a part of her world. But Belle and Caro were a package deal—so he had to somehow convince Belle that the three of them belonged together.

He glanced at Belle, standing behind the refreshment counter, helping Caro take the paper off her cupcake. He smiled to himself. The two of them were so beautiful it was hard not to look. The buzz of conversations, the ripples of laughter seemed to drift away. He was so caught up in watching them, he didn't even notice Chance walking up alongside him.

"You're making plans, aren't you?" he asked.

"What?" Caught, Wes looked at him.

"It's all right," Chance said, shoving his hands

into his pockets. "See, there's a look in your eye when you look at my sister that tells me I should back off. Let you two figure this out. So that's what I'm going to do."

"Glad to hear it," Wes said wryly, though he hadn't been the least bit worried about Chance Graystone or his brothers.

"Don't make me sorry." The man wandered over to Caro, scooped the girl up in his arms and gave her a spin that had giggles erupting and floating in the air like soap bubbles.

Wes watched and continued to plan. That little girl was his. Her mother was his, too. She just didn't know it yet.

But she would, soon.

By the time they got back to Belle's house, Caro was wired on sugar and excitement and getting her ready for bed was a challenge Wes was happy to leave to Belle. While they were upstairs, he went out to his car to get the surprise he'd had sent in from Texas. He'd called his company three days ago to order it, and tonight was the perfect time to give it to Caroline.

The now familiar house was quiet when he went back inside and headed up the stairs to his daughter's bedroom. But as he approached the open door, he heard Belle and the little girl talking. Shadows thrown from the night-lights plugged in at intervals along the hall crouched in corners. The old house sighed in the cold wind whipping under the eaves.

Moving quietly, he stopped in the doorway and blatantly eavesdropped.

"Is Wes gonna kiss me good-night?"

"He'll be here in a minute, sweetie."

"He's nice," Caro said, and though he couldn't see her, he imagined her small hands moving with every word, and his heart swelled.

"Yes, he is nice," Belle said, and Wes couldn't help but wonder if it had cost her to agree with her daughter.

"He's funny, too, and pretty and I think he should stay here now."

"Here?" Belle asked. "In Swan Hollow?"

"Here with us, Mommy," Caro answered and Wes went perfectly still, waiting to hear the rest. "He likes me and he should be here so we can play some more."

"Wes lives in Texas, honey," Belle said gently. "He's just visiting us."

"He's gonna *leave*?" There was a catch in Caro's throat that Wes felt as well.

"Not right away," Belle reassured her daughter, "but yes, he'll have to go home soon."

"But he can be home here, Mommy."

"It's not that easy, baby."

"Why?"

"Because…" She paused, clearly searching for an explanation that would make sense to a little girl. "…because his house is in Texas."

"Why?"

"Because that's where he lives."

"But *why*?"

He muffled a snort. He really shouldn't be enjoying so much how Belle squirmed, Wes thought. Still, he couldn't help the deep pang of regret he felt at making his little girl unhappy. It only strengthened his resolve to stay in her life permanently.

"Can we go to Texas?" Caro asked, trying a new tack.

Another long pause, and Wes imagined that Belle was wishing he would hurry and show up to dig her out of the conversation.

"No, we really can't."

"Why?"

He heard Isabelle sigh.

"What about your uncles? They all live here. Wouldn't you miss them?"

"Yes. But they could come, too!"

Wes felt a surge of pride. It seemed his daughter was as hardheaded as he was.

"Baby girl," Belle said, "how about we just enjoy Wes while he's here, okay?"

"But I don't want him to leave."

Wes's heart filled and he had to gulp in a breath to steady himself.

"I know, sweetie," Belle said softly. "Neither do I."

And he smiled. There it was. She didn't want him to leave any more than Caro did. So maybe it wouldn't be hard to convince Belle to come back to Texas with him. To try being together—not just for the sake of their daughter.

And on that happy thought, he stepped into Caroline's room. It was a little girl's dream, he imagined.

Everything from a canopy bed to a play table and chairs and bookcases filled with stories to be read over and over again. There were stuffed animals, a child's learning computer and, in the corner, a dollhouse as tall as Caro herself.

"Wes!" Caroline scooted out of bed, ran to him and threw her arms around his legs.

There went that twist to his heart again. While he hugged his daughter, his gaze caught Belle's, and he knew she was wondering how much of their conversation he'd overheard.

"Did you bring a present?" Caro squealed, her fingers moving as fast her voice. "For me?"

"It's a present for the best dancer in the whole show," he said, tapping his finger against his mouth. "Now who was that?"

"Me!" Caroline shouted. "It was me. Wasn't it me?" she asked, now sounding a little less confident.

"You bet it was you," Wes told her and handed her the red ribbon–wrapped white box.

"Mommy, look!" Caro staggered toward her mother, balancing the box awkwardly but refusing to put it down.

"I see," Belle said, laughing. "Why don't you put the box down so you can open it?"

"I will!" Caro set it on the floor, plopped down beside it and yanked at the ribbon until it fell away. Then she lifted the lid, pushed back the white tissue and said, "Ooh…"

One small word drawn out into a sigh of pleasure so rich and deep. Wes had to grin. She liked it.

"Mommy, *look*!" Caroline pulled the doll out of the box and inspected every inch of her. "She's like me, Mommy. Her hair and her eyes and, Mommy, she gots *hearing aids* like me!"

"You like her?" Wes asked unnecessarily.

"I *love* her," Caro said and handed the doll to her mother so she could run at Wes again. This time, he scooped her up and held her so she could throw her small arms around his neck and hang on. He'd never felt anything as wonderful as a freely given hug from his child. Her warm, soft weight in his arms, the scent of her shampoo, her grip on his neck and her whisper of "Thank you, Wes" made his heart fill to bursting.

Then he looked at Belle and saw her beautiful eyes shining with unshed tears and he was lost completely. He felt the ground beneath his feet shift as if he were standing in an earthquake. These two females had shattered him without even trying. And he wasn't entirely sure it bothered him.

Once Caroline was tucked in with her new doll clutched tightly to her chest, Isabelle led Wes from the room and pulled the door almost closed behind them.

In the dimly lit hallway, she turned to look up at Wes and said softly, "She loves that doll. Thank you."

"You don't have to thank me. But I'm glad she loves it." He smiled and threw a quick glance at the door separating them from their daughter. He looked back at Isabelle. "It's from our new Just Like Me line.

We're set to launch in a few weeks, so Caro got one of the very first."

The fact that he'd thought of it, arranged to have the doll sent here, touched Isabelle so deeply, her heart ached. "It meant so much to her. To me, too. You could have told her then. That you're her father."

He shook his head slowly. "No. I don't want to give her a present and a responsibility all at once. When I tell her who I am, I want it to be the right time."

Tears still brimmed in her eyes, remembering her daughter's excitement and the wonder on her face when she realized the doll had hearing aids just like she did. Wes could not have given her anything that would have meant more. It was hard on a child, being different from all of the other kids, but Caro was so much a force of nature, that even at four, she was completely sure of herself. And yet, having a doll with hearing aids had suddenly given Caro a boost of even more self-confidence.

Wes had given their daughter more than a doll. He'd given her acceptance. Now, with his simple truth that he wanted to wait for the right time to admit to Caroline who he was, Isabelle's heart was lost. Again.

She took a breath, grabbed Wes's hand, pulled him along the hallway and said, "Come with me."

"Where we going?"

"Where we were always headed," she said and tugged him into her bedroom. No point in lying to herself, Isabelle thought. This had been inevitable from the moment he arrived in Colorado. She'd known it, felt it. As if seeing him again had fanned every ember inside her into life, now that banked fire was a raging inferno and she didn't want to try to quench it anymore.

Moonlight on snow reflected into the room through the wide windows, giving the bedroom a soft, pale glow. She took a quick glance around the familiar space, the mountains of pillows stacked against the curved brass headboard, the thick, dark green comforter, the cozy chairs in front of the bay window and the brightly flowered rug across the gleaming wood floors. Reaching out, she flipped a wall switch and the gas fireplace in the sky blue–tiled hearth leaped to life.

This was her sanctuary. She'd never invited a man into this space before—not only because she hadn't been interested, but because she hadn't wanted Caroline to watch men coming and going. Not that there would have been a parade of men or anything. Yet tonight, it somehow seemed inevitable that Wes would be the first. Isabelle wasn't nervous, because it felt too right to her to second-guess herself. She'd made her decision and wouldn't back down now.

"Belle?" Wes looked down at her, desire warring with questions in his eyes.

"No talking," she said and went up on her toes. She hooked her arms around his neck, tipped her head to one side and kissed him with everything she had.

Surprised, it took him a second to react, but then

he was kissing her back, making Isabelle's head spin when he deepened that kiss, stealing her breath. He parted her lips with his tongue, dipping into her mouth to taste, explore with a hunger that matched her own.

His arms came around her, pressing her body tightly to his. Isabelle felt like she was on a roller coaster. Her stomach pitched wildly, her heartbeat thundered in her chest and everywhere he touched her, her skin burned.

One of his big hands caught the back of her head and his fingers speared through her hair, holding her still for the wild plundering of her mouth. She felt every inch of his body along hers and moaned at the hard length of him pushing against her abdomen. She wanted him, maybe more now than she ever had before.

She hadn't been with a man since Wes. Isabelle had told herself that she simply wasn't ready. That one day she would be and then she would move on. Find a life. But the simple truth was, she hadn't been able to be with another man because it was always Wes that she wanted. Everything she'd once felt for him came rushing back in an undeniable wave, knocking her sideways while she struggled to find balance.

Wes walked her forward a few steps, eased her onto the bed and then followed her down. He never let go of her, only adjusting his grip so that his hands could slide over her body with a fierce possessiveness that thrilled Isabelle. Finally, he tore his mouth from hers and she gasped and gulped for air.

Tipping her head back into the mattress, she felt him tugging at the buttons of her shirt and wished wildly for Velcro closing. It would be so much faster. At that last thought, the fabric parted and his hand came down on one of her breasts. Even through the silky lace of her bra, she felt the heat of him, and when his thumb rubbed across her nipple, she whimpered.

"Wes…"

"No talking," he whispered. "Remember?"

"Right. No talking. All I'll say is…*more*."

"Right there with you," he muttered and flicked open the front clasp of her bra, freeing her breasts so that he could lower his head and take first one nipple and then the other into his mouth.

Everything inside her exploded. Isabelle arched into him as his lips, tongue and teeth pulled at her sensitive nipples. A kaleidoscope of sensation shattered inside her mind. While he tortured her with his mouth, he slid one hand down her body to the waistband of her slacks, and in seconds he had the button and zipper undone. His fingers slipped beneath her panties to stroke her center.

And just like that, she was wearing too many clothes. Isabelle's mind struggled for clarity, even as her body shrieked at her to stop thinking and just feel. But she needed more of him. The hot slide of skin to skin, the feel of his hard, muscular body pressed to hers. The amazing sensation of him pushing into her depths and filling her completely.

"I want to feel you," she whispered.

He lifted his head and grinned. "You are."

She laughed a little and felt it tremble through her. "Funny. But take your clothes off."

"Yes, ma'am," he said, bending down to plant another long, hard kiss on her mouth.

She loved the taste of him, the feel of him. And when he moved away from her to peel off his clothes, she missed his warmth, the heat of their bodies wrapped together. He stood up, and she shrugged out of her clothes, kicked her pants off and lay on the comforter, watching him. When he stopped dead, with his hands at his belt, she managed to ask, "What's wrong?"

"We can't do this."

"What?"

He pushed both hands through his hair in frustration. "No protection, Belle. I haven't kept a condom in my wallet since I was in college."

She was glad to hear it. But she laughed a little and said, "Oh. For a second there, I thought you were changing your mind."

"Not a chance," he said, "but unless you—"

"In the bedside table drawer," she said, wanting to cut this conversation short and get back to shivering and trembling.

He pulled the drawer open, then looked at her, eyebrows arched. "Quite the supply," he said. "Been busy?"

She shook her head, licked her lips and choked out a short chuckle. "No. I think of that drawer as my hope chest. I figured it's better to have them and not need them—"

"Than to need them and not have them," he finished for her.

"Exactly."

He grabbed one of the foil packets, stripped out of his clothes and said, "I do like a woman who's prepared."

"Show me."

He didn't need another invitation. He came to her, covering her body with his, and Isabelle sighed at the first soft, warm contact of his skin to hers. She'd missed this so much. His scent, his taste, his strength. He was a businessman, but his big hands still carried the calluses he'd earned as a young man. And the scrape of his rough palms along her body created a new and even more exciting layer of sensation.

He rolled over, bringing her on top of him, and she loved looking down into those sea-colored crystal eyes. His hands cupped and kneaded her behind and she writhed on top of him in response. She kissed him hard, fast, then raised her head to watch him as she shifted, rising up, moving to straddle him.

In the moonlit room, even the air felt like magic. This moment was one she'd been thinking and dreaming of since she'd first opened her door and seen him on her porch. Slowly sitting up, she dragged the palms of her hands across his chest and loved the flash of something hot and dark that shot through his eyes.

Isabelle felt a rush of sexual power that ratcheted higher and higher inside her as she went up on her knees and slowly, slowly, lowered herself onto him. She took his hard, thick length inside, inch by glorious inch, and when he was filling her completely, she sighed and reveled in everything she was feeling.

He reached up, covering her breasts with his hands, tweaking and tugging at her nipples until she groaned and twisted her body in response. That movement sent shock waves rippling through her system and made her want to feel more, to feel it all.

Unable to wait a moment longer to experience the release clamoring inside her, Isabelle moved on him, rocking up and down in a slow, rhythmic dance that created tingles that rose up and burst and rose up again. She lifted her arms high over her head, giving herself over to what was happening, and the feel of his hands on her breasts only fed the fire that burned brightly inside her.

Then his hands dropped to her hips and guided her into a faster pace. His gaze locked on hers, they stared into each other's eyes as they claimed each other in the most intimate way possible. The tingle at her core became an incessant burn that ached and ached, pushing her toward the release she needed. And when Isabelle felt she couldn't take it a moment more, the needing, the desire, he shifted one hand to her center and rubbed that sensitive nub at her core.

"Wes!" She cried his name but kept moving on

him, kept rocking, twisting her hips in a blind effort to take him higher, deeper. That bone-deep ache intensified as they moved together in a dance as ancient as time, and when her body exploded, shattering into a fusillade of color and sensation, Isabelle clung to his forearms and rode the wave to the end.

Only then, when she was shaking and shivering, did Wes let himself follow. She stared into his eyes and watched as he surrendered himself to her. Gave himself to her.

And she wished, from the bottom of her heart, that that surrender was complete.

Seven

An hour later, they were lying wrapped together beneath the comforter. There was a bottle of wine on the nightstand, thanks to Wes making a trip down to the kitchen. He'd had to wait until he was sure his legs would work—but he'd needed those few minutes away from Belle. Away from what they'd shared, to try to think. Hopeless, though, since there wasn't enough blood flow to fuel his brain. All he knew was that what he'd just shared with Belle had been so much more than he'd expected. So much more than he'd been ready for. He'd have to take the time—later—to examine it all from every possible angle. But for now, he was only hoping to experience it all again. Soon.

Outside, snow fell again in soft, white puffs that

danced against the window and slid down the glass. Inside, the room was warm, the wine was cold and firelight tossed dancing shadows across the walls.

"Well," Belle said on a sigh, "that was…"

Wes smiled to himself, then took a sip of his wine. "Yeah, it was."

Belle tugged the edge of the comforter up to cover her breasts as she leaned back on the pillows propped against the brass headboard. Then she pushed one hand through her hair and sipped at her own wine. "So, do we need to talk about this?"

Why did women always want to *talk*? He grinned and shrugged. "We're both naked, lying here drinking wine, and I don't know about you, but I'm already thinking about round two. What is there to talk about?"

She shifted, sliding one leg over his. "Well, I thought I should try to explain why we had round one."

He ran his hand over her thigh and smiled when she shivered. Wes didn't want her thinking too much about any of this. Better that they simply accept what happened and build on it. Why ask too many questions? The answers might not be what either of them wanted to hear.

"Oh, no explanation necessary." He winked and said, "I understand completely. You couldn't fight off your desire for me any longer, and in a rush of lust, you surrendered to the urge to fling yourself into my manly arms."

She blinked at him, then smiled, then laughed as she shook her head. "You're crazy."

"That's been said before," he told her and moved, taking her wineglass and setting it on the table beside his. He wanted her off balance with no time to think, to consider, to second-guess the decision she'd already made. Because there was more that he wanted and now that he'd made this much headway, he didn't want to backslide.

He cupped her face in his palm, stared into her eyes and said, "I have to go back to Texas, Belle. Tomorrow. The day after, at the latest."

Surprise flickered in her eyes. She covered his hand with hers. "You're leaving?"

"I have to get back." That was true. His company was trying to fight its way out of a scandal. He had to try to save that merger. And they were getting ready for the big toy launch. And that was just dealing with TTG. He had any number of other companies he had to check on. "There are things I have to be on-site to handle. I've already stayed longer than I should have—not that I'm sorry about that. But I've got to get back."

Her eyes mirrored what she was thinking. They always had. That's why he had known five years ago that she was falling for him. Why he'd let her go. And why right now, he knew she didn't want him to leave.

"Caro will miss you."

He kissed her. "Only Caro?"

She sighed. "I will, too, damn it."

He laughed, enjoying the irritation on her face. "I can fix that. Come with me."

She blinked at him. "To *Texas*?"

"Why not?"

"How many reasons do you need?" She inched away from him, scooted higher on the pillows and pushed her hair back from her face again.

"Come for a week, Belle." He talked fast, knowing he had to drive his point home and make it count. "Come home with me. Let me show Caroline where I live, let her see some of Texas."

"I can't just pick up and go, Wes."

She wasn't saying no outright, so that gave him some wiggle room. He'd take it. "Give me a reason why not. One good one. We'll start there."

"Caro's school."

He almost laughed. "Pre-K, Belle," he said, shaking his head at the sad attempt at an excuse. "It's not like she's in med school. You could pull her out for a week. Call it an extended field trip."

She scowled at him, clearly realizing that she hadn't offered much of a reason. A second later, she tried again. "Fine. Then there's my work. I have donations to line up, plans to finalize..."

He was prepared for that argument, too. Wes had been thinking about this for a few days now, and tonight had sealed it all in his mind. He had to go back home, and he wasn't going to leave alone.

"And in Texas, you can visit the company, meet with the PR team, and they'll help you come up with ways to drum up more donations."

"I don't need help—"

"And," he interrupted, "you can go through the toy catalog at the company and choose which toys of ours you want to add to your project."

"I hate when you interrupt me."

"I know. Maybe that's why I do it." He gave her another smile and she rolled her eyes.

Then she bit her lip and her gaze slid from his as if she didn't want him to see what she was thinking. He knew she was considering it, and he also knew enough to let his adversary work through everything without another interruption. *Adversary.* That word stuck in his brain until he mentally erased it. She wasn't an enemy. She was—hell, he wasn't completely sure what Belle was to him. He only knew that he wasn't ready to be without her.

"Say we do go with you. Then what?" she finally asked, her voice little more than a whisper.

"What do you mean?"

She half turned on the bed to meet his gaze. Firelight played over her skin and flickered in her eyes. "I mean, say we spend the week together, all of us. What happens after that? Caro and I come back home, you stay in Texas and we all go on with our lives like before?"

He smoothed her hair back, more because he couldn't stop himself from touching her than for any other reason. His fingertips traced along her jawline then dropped to where her hand lay on the comforter. He took it in his and held on. He thought about it for a second, considered his options, then went with honesty.

"I don't know, Belle. Neither of us *can* know. All I'm sure of is that I want you and Caro to come with me. To be with me. Give me that week, Belle."

Her gaze never wavered. She looked at him for several long, tense seconds as if trying to see past his reserve to what he was really thinking. If she knew, he told himself, she would never come with him.

He wanted her in Texas not only because he wanted more time with Caro. Not only because he wanted Belle in his bed. But because if the three of them presented a united front, the scandal driven by Maverick might disappear entirely and Teddy Bradford could get back on board with the merger.

His people were no closer to finding the mysterious Maverick, but he had learned that Bradford wasn't in talks with anyone else. So the odds of him being in on the scandal eruption were really low. And that meant that the merger might still be salvageable. If he worked this right.

He swallowed his impatience and let Belle see only what he wanted her to see. A man unwilling to let go just yet.

Finally, she nodded. "Okay. A week. After that, we'll talk about what comes next."

He squeezed her hand and smiled. "We'll work something out," he promised her and meant it. No matter what else happened in his life, he knew he'd find a way to keep Caro, and maybe her mother, in his life.

She smiled, but it was barely more than a slight lifting of her lips. Wes knew she wasn't sure of this decision, but he wasn't going to give her a chance to change her mind, either.

"Good," he said, leaning in to kiss her. "Now that that's settled…" He pushed the comforter down and cupped her breast, thumb and forefinger rubbing her hardened nipple until her eyes glazed over and she gave a soft sigh. Smiling down into her eyes, he quipped, "I think it's time to think about round two. I'm feeling the need to fling myself at you. How do you feel about that?"

She held his hand to her breast and with her free hand she reached up and drew his face to hers. "Fling when ready."

He grinned. Damned if he hadn't missed her. He hadn't allowed himself to acknowledge it before now. He remembered all the nights they'd stayed awake talking, laughing, making love. He'd never had that in his life until Belle, and when she left Texas, she'd taken all of it with her.

No other woman had given him what she had. Now she was back in his life, and he wasn't going to let her go anytime soon.

He bent his head to kiss her and instantly lost all thought under the rising tide of need. Tomorrow could take care of itself. For tonight, all he wanted was *this*.

Two days later, the three of them were on Wes's private jet. Edna had urged her to go, to see where this thing with Wes would lead, and with that tiny bit of encouragement, Isabelle was going to give it a try. Of course, it didn't help anything to know that Chance, Eli and Tyler were less than thrilled at her going off with Wes. Though they'd changed their initial opinion of him mainly because of the way he was with Caro, Isabelle's brothers were still not ready to trust him not to hurt her or her daughter.

Neither was she, when it came right down to it. But if she didn't try, she'd never forgive herself. Still, Isabelle knew she had to approach this time with Wes carefully. If not to protect her own heart—then at least to guard Caroline's.

Because her little girl was thrilled with this new adventure. Caro loved the plane, loved flying above the clouds and loved the limo ride from the airport to Wes's home just west of Royal, Texas.

Five years ago, Wes had been in the process of building his home. Isabelle had seen the blueprints, they'd talked about different design features and she'd suggested quite a few changes to the original plan. Now, seeing it finished, Isabelle thought it was breathtaking.

Under the soft Texas winter sun, the massive two-story house sprawled across a beautifully landscaped property. There was a tidy lawn that seemed wider than a football field. Young trees ran the perimeter of the property with a few older live oak trees that had been left standing during construction. Flowers in wildly bright and cheerful colors hugged the base of the house and lined the brick walk that led to the long, inviting porch.

The house itself was a gorgeous blend of wood and stone and glass. Tall windows lined the front of the house and glinted in the sunlight. Stone walls made the house look as if it had been standing in that spot for decades. The porch was filled with rocking chairs and a swing that hung by thick chains from the overhead beams. A white wood railing completed that picture, along with the baskets of flowers that stood at either side of the double front doors.

Isabelle was used to seeing mountains, and the land here was flat, but for a few rolling hills in the distance. And still, it was beautiful.

It seemed strange, Isabelle thought. They'd left Colorado in the middle of the latest snowstorm. There were snowdrifts four feet high all over Swan Hollow. And here in Texas, there were winter flowers blooming under a mild sun. Kind of a culture shock for Isabelle, but Caroline didn't seem to have a problem with it.

The little girl, clutching her new favorite doll, bolted from the limo onto the grass. She spun in a circle, holding her head back and laughing. When she stopped, she looked at her mother, wide-eyed. "There's no snow, Mommy!"

"I know, baby." Isabelle tossed a glance at Wes to see him smiling indulgently. Looking back to Caro, she asked, "Do you like it?"

"I like making snowmen," she said thoughtfully,

taking another slow spin to look all around her. "But I like this, too."

"I'm glad you do," Wes said, using sign language as well as speaking. "We don't have snow, but we have other fun stuff."

"Like what?" Caroline asked, eyes bright and interested.

Put on the spot, he seemed to flounder for a minute and Isabelle waited, curious to see how he'd recover. She shouldn't have doubted him.

"Oh, we've got a big zoo that has a carousel and we've got lakes. We can go out on a boat—"

"I like boats!" Caroline grinned. "Uncle Chance has a boat and it's fun!"

"Good to know," Wes said wryly. "There's an amusement park in Houston where we can go on rides, and there's a trampoline park, too." He reached out and gently tugged one of her pigtails. "Texas has a lot of great stuff."

"But no snow."

He shook his head. "Not usually."

She thought about that for a second then shrugged. "It's okay. Home has snow, so it's okay you don't."

"Well, thanks," Wes said, slanting a look at Isabelle. "You know, your mom used to live in Texas."

"Really?" She looked up at her mother. "Did you have fun with Wes, too?"

Before she answered, she saw the speculative expression on Wes's face and smiled to herself. The man was impossible. "I sure did, honey. So will you."

At least, Isabelle really hoped so. Looking at her

little girl's excitement right now, she could only pray that nothing happened to dampen that enthusiasm. Shifting her gaze to Wes, Isabelle tried to see beyond the facade to the man beneath. What did this trip mean to him? Was it simply to get a little extra time with his daughter? Was he considering a future for all of them? Or was there another reason for this trip altogether? Impossible to know.

"Why don't we go inside," Wes said to Caroline. "Then you can see your room."

"*My* room?" Caro asked, her mouth wide-open in pleased surprise.

"Yep, and it's special just for you." He took Caroline's hand, winked at Isabelle, then walked to the front door, the little girl skipping and chattering happily alongside him.

Isabelle followed, shaking her head. The man never ceased to surprise her. Of course he had a room for Caroline. He'd had two days, after all. No doubt he'd made a few calls and had everything taken care of just the way he wanted it. It probably should have bothered her that he was so obviously planning on more than just a week with Caroline. You didn't go to that kind of trouble for a child who would only be spending a few days there. But on the other hand, how could she be upset with a man who went the extra mile to make their daughter feel special?

"A dog! You gots a dog!"

Caroline's squeal of delight reached Isabelle as she stepped up onto the porch, and she couldn't quite hold back a sigh of defeat. Caro had been asking for a dog for months, and Isabelle had kept putting her off. Now Caroline would be even more determined than ever.

Isabelle stepped into the entryway and immediately noted the warm oak floors, the pale misty-green walls and the thick oak trim everywhere. There was a table near the stairs where a vase of flowers stood and several doors leading off a long hallway that stretched to the back of the house. Later, she'd have time to explore. But for right now, Isabelle's gaze was fixed on her daughter and the golden retriever currently adoring each other.

"What's his name?" Caro demanded as she buried her face in all that soft, golden fur.

"Her name is Abbey," Wes said, signing as well as speaking.

Isabelle had to admit that his signing had really come a long way in a week. Clearly he was practicing a lot.

Abbey, reacting to her name, abandoned Caroline briefly to welcome Wes home, her nails clicking on the hardwood floor. Then the big dog shifted her attention to Isabelle, coming up to her and leaning against her, giving Isabelle the opportunity to stroke that sleek golden head. But when the hellos were done, the dog shot straight back to Caroline. She plopped to the floor in front of the little girl and rolled over to her back to allow for a good belly rub. Caro complied with a delighted laugh.

"I like dogs," Caro shouted over her own laughter when Abbey sprang up to lick the girl's face.

"She likes you, too," Wes said, then as an older woman approached, said, "I'm home, Bobbi."

"So I see." Bobbi had long, gray-streaked black hair, currently in a thick braid that hung over one shoulder. She wore jeans, a long-sleeved blue T-shirt and dark red cowboy boots. "You brought me a little girl to spoil, too, I see."

"Hi," the girl announced. "I'm Caroline."

"Nice to meet you," Bobbi said. Then, holding out a hand, she said, "You must be Isabelle."

"I am, it's nice to meet you, too." Isabelle looked around, then back to the woman who was so clearly in charge. "It's a gorgeous house."

"Needs some life in it," Bobbi pointed out with a slanted look at Wes. "But looks like it'll be a little livelier for a while anyway."

"All right," Wes said, tossing a knowing look at the older woman. "Caro, you want to see your room? It's upstairs."

Bobbi's eyebrows lifted at the sign language he used, but then she nodded as if pleased to see it.

"I do! Come on, Abbey!" Caroline headed for the stairs at a run, and the dog was only a pace behind her.

Isabelle and Wes followed, and when he took her hand, she held on, pleased at the warmth. The connection. This was a big step for her. Coming back to Royal with the man she had once run from. Odd that she'd never planned on it, but she'd ended up coming full circle. If it all worked out somehow, great. If it didn't, would she pay for this decision for the rest of her life? For her own sake, as well as Caroline's, she hoped not.

At the top of the stairs, they turned left and Wes led the way to a door halfway down the hall. When he threw it open, Caroline raced inside, then stopped dead and sighed, "Oh, boy."

Isabelle had to agree. Wes had gone all out. The room was a pale, dreamy blue, with white curtains at the windows and a blue-and-white coverlet on the bed. There was a table and chairs in one corner, bookshelves filled with books and a child-size blue couch covered in white pillows, just made for curling up and daydreaming. There was a mural on the wall of butterflies, fairies and storybook castles and a thick blue rug spread across the wood floors.

How he'd managed all of this in just a couple of days was amazing. Unless, Isabelle thought with a sideways glance at him, he'd been planning to get her and Caro to Texas all along. Good thing? Bad? She couldn't be sure yet.

Caroline whipped around, still clutching her doll in the crook of one arm, and threw her free arm around Wes's knees. Tipping her head back, she said, softly, "Thank you, Wes."

He cupped the back of her head and smiled down at her with a gentleness that touched Isabelle's heart. There were so many layers to the man that she doubted she would ever learn them all. But this man, the gentle, loving man, was the one she'd fallen so deeply in love with years ago. It was a side of him she'd rarely seen, and it was all the more beautiful now because of it.

And Isabelle was forced to admit, at least to herself, that she *still* loved him. Watching him with their daughter had only solidified the feelings that had never faded away. She'd known five years ago, even when she left him, that she wouldn't be able to run far enough to outdistance what she felt for him. She'd tried. She'd buried herself in work she believed in, in caring for her daughter and in being a part of her town and her family.

But in spite of everything, for five long years, Wes had remained in the back of her mind, in a corner of her heart. And even as she tried to fool herself, she'd known somehow that what she felt for him was still alive and well. Today just proved that.

As her heart ached and her throat tightened, he lifted his head, catching her eye, and everything inside her melted. Isabelle had risked a lot by coming here with him, staying with him. But it was too late to back out now. She had to see this through. See where it would take her. Love didn't disappear just because it was inconvenient. But if she walked away a second time with a broken heart, Isabelle wasn't sure she'd survive it.

"You're welcome," he said to the little girl still beaming at him as if he were a superhero.

Caroline gave him another quick grin, then climbed onto her couch to try it out and Abbey crawled up right beside her, laying her big head in the little girl's lap. Clearly, a mutual adoration society had been born.

"Now," Wes said to Isabelle, "I'll show you your room." He took her hand again to lead her directly across the hall.

The moment he opened the door, she knew it was the master bedroom. It was massive. Far bigger than her own bedroom at home, this one boasted a stone fireplace on one wall, with a flat-screen TV mounted over the mantel. There were two comfy high-back chairs and a small table in front of the hearth, and on either side of the fireplace, floor-to-ceiling bookcases. A bank of windows on the far wall was bare of curtains and displayed a view of the trees, grass, a swimming pool and those hills she'd spotted before, off in the distance. There was also what looked like a barn. Or a stable.

She wondered idly how many acres he owned, but then her thoughts were scattered by a glance at his bed. It was *huge*. A dark blue duvet lay atop the mattress, and the head and footboard were heavy golden oak. Dark red rugs were tossed across the shining floor, and all in all, it was a beautiful, masculine space. But it was the bed that kept drawing her gaze. Finally she forced herself to look away, to meet Wes's gaze.

In his eyes, she saw the glint of desire and the determination of a man who knew what he wanted and had no trouble going after it. "You don't have another guest room?"

He gave her a half smile, reached out and stroked

one hand down her back. Isabelle took a breath, then steeled herself against her reaction. The ripple of goose bumps along her arms, mixed with the heat building at her core, was enough to shatter any woman's defenses.

"Sure," he said, voice a low rumble of need, "but we can't pretend we didn't sleep together. Can't go back, Belle." His gaze locked on hers. "And I wouldn't even if we could. Don't think you would, either."

She shook her head. No point in denying it.

"Do you really want us to be sneaking up and down the hallway in the middle of the night?"

The image his words painted was both pitiful and funny. She sighed. "With Caro right across the hall…"

Wes chuckled. "She won't think anything of it, Belle. Heck, with Abbey around, she probably won't *notice*." He moved in and wrapped both arms around her. "We already crossed this bridge back in Colorado, you know. You're not going to try to tell me you're sorry about it, are you?"

No, she really wasn't. Maybe she should have been, but she wasn't. Five years without him had been long and lonely. Having him back in her life might be dangerous to her heart, but Isabelle knew that loving him was no longer a choice for her. It just *was*.

As for sharing his bed here… Isabelle would be going to bed long after Caro. And she'd be up before her daughter in the morning, so her little girl would probably never realize where her mother was spending the night. And honestly, Isabelle admitted silently, she wanted to stay with Wes. She was here for a week. Why not enjoy what she had while she had it? Risk be damned. If this time with him was destined to end, Isabelle at least wanted *now*.

"No," she said, "I'm not sorry." She watched pleasure dart across his eyes, then she lifted one hand and cupped his cheek, just because she wanted to. "I'll stay here. With you."

"Good." He caught her hand and held onto it. "Now that we've got that settled…come on."

Frowning at his abrupt shift, she asked, "Where are we going?"

"Outside. Let's find out if Caro likes her pony."

"What?" She laughed as he pulled her along behind him and wondered how she'd ever made it through the last five years without him.

Eight

"Boss?" Robin's voice was a little loud, which made Wes think this wasn't the first time she'd spoken to him.

Whatever the situation going on at home, he had to focus here at work. "Sorry. Yeah. What were you saying?"

She frowned at him. "Everything all right?"

"Sure." He pushed up from his desk, stood straight and shoved his hands into his pockets. "So what's going on?"

She didn't look like she believed him, but since he was the boss, she went with it. "Okay, the news from Texas Tech is good," she said. "They've got the next line of tablets ready to roll before summer, with the new bells and whistles you ordered."

"Good." He moved out from behind his desk and walked to the window overlooking the city of Houston. While the PR and IT teams were still working on uncovering the mysterious Maverick, Wes was concentrating on the other arms of Jackson Inc. He had majority interest in Texas Tech; Texas Jets, a charter jet service; and a few other smaller yet growing companies. He'd been building his empire for decades, and getting to the bottom of Maverick's deliberate sabotage of Texas Toy Goods was important. He couldn't risk the man going after any of his other companies as well.

"I want to talk to Sam Holloway at Texas Jets sometime today," he said, never taking his gaze from the cityscape sprawled out below him. "And then get me Andy at Texas Tech. I want to hear details on those bells and whistles."

"Got it."

He half turned from the window. "Are Belle and Caroline still in the PR department?"

"Isabelle is, yes," Robin told him. "But Maggie from PR took Caroline down to the cafeteria for a chocolate shake." She sighed and smiled. "That little girl is just adorable, boss. I gotta say, makes me miss my own kids' younger days."

"Yeah, she's pretty great," he said, thinking, as he had been for days now, about how Caroline had wormed her way straight into his heart, and no matter what happened between him and Isabelle, nothing for him would ever be the same again.

"She showed me how to say hello in sign language." Robin shook her head. "Smart kid. Just like her daddy."

His eyebrows lifted.

"Please." Robin waved one hand at him. "No, you didn't make some grand announcement, but I'd have to be blind to not notice the child has your eyes. Right down to the unusual color."

"It's not a secret," he said, then half laughed at himself. "At least, not since Maverick blasted it all over the internet. But I haven't told Caro who I am yet."

"For heaven's sake, *why*?" Robin asked.

She sounded completely exasperated, and Wes realized that for some reason, his assistant and his housekeeper shared the same attitude. Neither of them was intimidated by him and both of them continually seemed to forget just who was really in charge. "You know, I could fire you," he pointed out wryly.

She waved that away with a flick of her hand. "That'll never happen and we both know it. So why haven't you told that child you're her father?"

"Because I want her to know me. To—" it was humiliating to admit "—*like* me."

Robin gave him an understanding smile. "She already does, boss. You can see it in the way her face lights up when you walk into the room."

He pushed his hand through his hair. Robin was right. He'd seen that look. It had made him feel ten feet tall. So why then was he waiting to tell his daughter who he really was? He hated to think it was fear. Hell, nothing had scared Wes in…well, ever. But the thought of that little girl turning from him could bring him to his knees.

"Robin," he said abruptly, "I'm taking the rest of the day off."

"I'm sorry. I think I must have had a stroke. What was that?"

"Surrounded by sarcasm," he said with a nod. "I'm taking the day off."

"Yesterday, you took Caroline to the aquarium, the day before it was ice-skating and the day before that you and Isabelle had her riding roller coasters." Robin tipped her head to one side and looked at him. "I'm beginning to think you might be looking for a life, boss."

"I'm beginning to think you may be right." He grinned and shrugged into his jacket. "Just forward my calls to my cell. I'll check messages later."

He caught up to Isabelle in PR. The room was bustling, people typing on keyboards, sketching on whiteboards and huddled around desks, arguing and discussing. The noise level was high, so Wes decided to try out some sign language. He caught her eye and from across the room, she smiled at him. Then she flushed and chuckled when he started signing.

At another desk, a guy named Drake laughed, too, then ducked his head and pretended he hadn't.

"Something funny?" Wes asked him.

"Um, no, sir," the kid answered quickly, his gaze darting from side to side to avoid making direct contact with Wes's. "It's just that, um, my mother's deaf. I speak sign language, and, well..."

"Perfect." Wes sighed and shook his head. "What were the odds," he muttered. Then he bent low and whispered, "I expect you to forget everything you just saw."

"Didn't see a thing," Drake assured him and deliberately went back to work with a frenzied attack on his keyboard.

Nodding, Wes was satisfied that the kid wouldn't be telling anyone that the boss had just signed, *You look incredible. I want you in bed. Now.*

Isabelle walked toward him, still smiling. He took her hand and led her from the room. Out in the hall, he said, "Well, that was unexpected. I didn't think there'd be someone here who understands sign language."

She squeezed his hand and let him see her smile grow. "It's okay. I don't think he's going to be telling anyone that you want me in bad."

He stopped. *"Bad?"*

Laughing, she nodded. "You're getting better at signing every day, but it's pretty tricky."

No wonder the kid had laughed. "Still, having you wrapped up in bed and bad on top of it isn't a bad idea, either. I could eat my way down to you and then just keep going."

Her eyes flashed and she licked her lips, sending a jolt of heat straight down to the one area of his body that hadn't relaxed since he'd first seen her. Shaking his head, he murmured, "I came to get you so we could take Caro to the zoo. But now..."

She tipped her head to his shoulder briefly, then looked up at him. "Zoo first. Bad later."

"Deal."

They must have walked for miles, Isabelle thought. She and Wes and Caroline had spent hours at the zoo, and she wouldn't have thought that Wes would enjoy it. But he had. Just as much as he'd enjoyed the amusement park and the ice-skating. Maybe it was the magic of seeing things through the eyes of a child, but he'd been more relaxed and happy in the last few days than she'd ever seen him. In a gray suit, now minus the red power tie, he should have looked out of place at the zoo. But she'd learned that Wes wasn't a man easily defined. Despite the suit, he carried Caro on his shoulders and didn't seem to mind when her ice cream cone dripped all over him. On the ride home to Royal, it took only seconds for Caro to be sound asleep in her car seat. After checking on her, Isabelle sat back and turned her head to look at Wes. Her heart did a quick tumble as she stared at his profile. "Caro had a wonderful time today."

He glanced at her and gave her a half smile. "So did I. Until this week, I hadn't taken a day off in years. I think Robin is shell-shocked."

Isabelle laughed. She'd always liked Wes's no-nonsense assistant. "She'll recover."

"How did it go in the PR department?" He paused.

"You know, before I got there. You get anything you can use?"

"Absolutely." In the couple of hours she'd been with PR that morning, Isabelle had found new and clever ways to hit people up for donations. "Mike actually suggested that I sort of adopt out hospitals."

"You lost me." He steered the car into the passing lane to go around a truck.

"Well—" she turned in her seat to face him even though he had to keep his eyes on the road "—it's like, I print up information on specific hospitals. The kids—first names only—their health issues, how long they'll be there in that sterile environment. Let potential donors see these kids as real people rather than just another random charity."

"Good idea." He nodded. "And you'd send these flyers or newsletters or whatever out to your mailing list?"

"To start, yes, but I could also make more of a splash on my Facebook page. And get more involved in social media. Honestly, I get so busy with the actual work that I forget I also have to get out there and promote what the charity does, too. Social media is so hot right now—"

"Believe me," Wes said with a tight groan, "I know."

"Right." She winced, remembering suddenly that it had been a Twitter attack that had brought them back together. "Sorry. Sore spot."

"It's okay," he said, shaking his head. "Go ahead."

"All right. So Mike suggested I start a public

Facebook page detailing what the nonprofit is about. Pictures of the toys we give to these kids. Maybe pictures of the toy closets in the hospitals themselves. I'd like to add pictures of the kids with their toys, but I'd have to get their parents to sign releases..."

"They probably would," he said.

"You think so?"

"You should know better than me what a parent of a sick kid would be feeling. What would you have done if someone had given Caro a brand-new doll or stuffed animal when she was miserable in the hospital?" He looked at her briefly.

"I'd have kissed them," she admitted. "So, okay, maybe you're right about that. I can check with some of the parents at the hospital when we go home next week and—"

"About that..."

She looked at him for a long second or two before saying, "What?"

"Well," he said, shifting position slightly in his seat, "I was just thinking that maybe one week here won't be enough time. I mean, for Caroline. To get to know me, my place—hell, Texas."

Isabelle frowned, and her stomach jumped with a sudden eruption of nerves. "We agreed on a week, Wes. I have work. Caro has school. We don't live here."

"You could."

"What are you saying?" Her heart jumped into her throat and the hard, rapid beat thundered in her ears. Was he saying what she thought he might be saying, because if he was, driving down the freeway doing eighty miles an hour was an odd time to be saying it. "You want us to *live* here?"

"Sure. The house is huge, plenty of room, Caro could go to school in Royal and—"

He kept talking, but Isabelle had stopped listening. There was no mention of love or commitment or anything else in that little speech. He wanted them in his house, her in his bed, but he was no closer to intimacy than he had been five years ago, so Isabelle did them both a favor and interrupted him. "Wes, it's really not the time to talk about this."

His mouth worked as if he were biting back words clamoring to get out. Finally though, he said, "Okay. But you can think about it."

She could practically guarantee she wouldn't be thinking about anything else. The fact that he could just bring up the idea so casually, though, told Isabelle more than she wanted to know. He wasn't looking for family. For love. He wanted her and Caro to be a part of his life without strings. Without the ties that would make them a unit.

Maybe she'd been fooling herself from the beginning.

"Okay," he said, still frowning, "we'll table that discussion for now. Instead, you can tell me if you got a chance to look through the toy catalog I gave you yesterday."

He went from frowning to facile in the blink of an eye. She'd forgotten he could do that. Isabelle used to be fascinated by the way he could switch gears so easily. If he saw himself losing one argument, he'd immediately change tacks and come at it from a completely different direction, and pretty soon, he had exactly what he'd wanted all along.

Now, he was doing it to *her*. Isabelle was going to keep her guard up around him, because he was her weakness. She couldn't let him see that she loved him, because one of two things would happen—he'd either back off as he had five years ago. Or, worse yet, he'd look at her with pity.

She wasn't interested in either.

"I did," she said, deliberately cheerful. "You've got some great things, Wes. If you're serious about donating, we'd love to add anything you can spare."

He reached over and took her hand, holding it in his much larger one. The heat of him swept up her arm to puddle in the center of her chest, wrapping her heart in the warmth of him. God, she wasn't going to be able to protect her heart, because it was already his.

"Just tell Robin what you need. She'll take care of it."

"Thanks." She couldn't stop looking at him. Maybe she was storing up memories, Isabelle thought. Maybe a part of her knew that this couldn't last and was instinctively etching him into her mind so that years from now, when she was still missing him, she could pull these images out and remember.

She only hoped it would be enough.

The following evening, Wes realized that he was in the middle of the very situation he'd been avoiding for years. He had a woman and a child in his home, and instead of feeling trapped, he felt…good.

But then, this wasn't permanent, was it? That thought didn't bring him the rush of happiness he would have expected. When he'd suggested to Belle that she and Caroline could stay with him, she hadn't jumped at it, had she? So he was still looking at saying goodbye to them all too soon. His guts twisted into knots. Isabelle had only agreed to be here for a week, and four of those days were already gone.

And instead of being at home with them right now, he was here at the Texas Cattleman's Club for a meeting. Shaking his head, he lifted the crystal tumbler in front of him and took a small sip of his scotch. Usually, he enjoyed coming into town, sitting in the lounge, talking with friends, joining in on plans for the future of the club. But tonight, he knew Isabelle and Caroline were back at the house, and he caught himself constantly wondering what they were up to while he was stuck here.

"Your head's not in this meeting," an amused voice noted.

Wes looked at Clay Everett and gave him a nod. "Good catch." Clay was a local rancher with brown hair, green eyes and a permanent limp due to a bull-riding accident. Like Wes, Clay was a driven, stubborn man.

"So what's more fascinating than painting the club restrooms?" Tom Knox asked.

"Oh, I don't know," Toby McKittrick said wryly. "*Everything*, maybe?"

Wes grinned and gazed at each of the men in turn. Tom looked the part of the ex-soldier he was, with broad shoulders, lots of tattoos and the scars he carried as a badge of honor. He was a man to be counted on.

Toby was taller, leaner and just as stubborn as the rest of them. A rancher, he was loyal to his friends, tough on his enemies and didn't take crap from any-one.

"Yeah, got better things to do than sit here and lis-ten to a lot of nonsense," Wes said, idly turning the scotch glass in damp circles on the tabletop.

"So I heard," Tom said with a knowing smile. "Isabelle's back. How's that going?"

"The word is," Clay offered slyly, "our boy Wes here is practically domesticated."

"No way," Toby put in with a laugh. "The woman who could put a leash on this man hasn't been born yet."

"Not what I hear," Clay said, taking a sip of his beer.

Great. Even his friends were talking about him, wondering about what was going on. He supposed bringing Isabelle and Caro back to Royal had been inviting the gossip, but what the hell else could he have done? Eventually, he knew, the talk in Royal would move on to some fresh meat and he and his problems would fade away. All he had to do was make it that long without popping someone in the mouth.

And he didn't have a damn leash around his neck.

Wes nodded as he lifted his glass to the other men. "Good to be with friends who know just how to aim their shots."

They all took a drink and Toby said, "Damn straight. What're friends for, after all? And since we're such good friends, maybe we should go back to your place with you. Let Isabelle know that when she gets tired of dealing with you, we stand at the ready."

Giving him a smile, Wes shook his head. "Yeah. That'll happen. I don't think so."

Clay grinned. "Worth a try. When do we meet your daughter, then?"

Wes shot him a look. He shouldn't have been surprised, since half the country had been talking about him, thanks to Maverick and Twitter. Still, it seemed weird to have someone ask about his *daughter* so easily.

"Soon," he said. "Hopefully. Her mother and I have some things to work out first. Which I could be at home doing if I wasn't here listening to the old-timers gripe about too many changes."

"The girl's a cutie," Clay told him. "Saw pictures of you three in the grocery store."

"What?" Wes just looked at his friend and waited.

"Yeah, those tabloids by the cash registers? There you all were at the ice-skating rink." Clay shrugged. "Headline was something like hashtag Deadbeatdad No More."

"Great. That's terrific."

"Hey," Toby said, "it's better than saying you're *still* a crappy father."

"I didn't know I was a father," Wes pointed out.

"Yeah, we know," Tom said, holding both hands up in mock surrender. "We're just saying that everybody else seeing the three of you looking like a family is going to take the sting out of that whole Twitter nonsense."

He had a point, Wes told himself. And if the pictures were in the tabloids, they'd be showing up other places, too. Magazines, newspapers, online. Teddy Bradford would see them and maybe rethink his position on the merger. One of the reasons Wes had brought Isabelle and Caroline back to Texas with him was to take the pressure off the scandal.

So why was he feeling a little guilty about all of this now?

Wes scanned the room, noting the members who were here and wondering about those who weren't. Hell, it was a pain in the butt to have to come to redecorating meetings, but if you were a member you should damn well show up and do what needed doing.

The club had been the same for more than a hundred years. Typical of the wealthy, men-only clubs of the day, the TCC had mostly been decorated with masculine comfort in mind. Hunting trophies along with historical Texas documents and pictures dotted the walls. Dark beams crossed the ceilings, which were higher now, thanks to the renovations done after damage incurred by the last tornado. The furniture was dark leather, a blaze burned in the stone fireplace and the thick rugs that were spread across the gleaming wood floor were a deep red.

Of course, since female members were admitted to the club several years ago, there'd been some changes, too. The child care facility was the most monumental, but there were smaller, less obvious changes as well. The walls were a lighter color, there were fresh flowers in the meeting rooms and the quiet hush that used to define the old place had been replaced with an abundance of feminine voices.

Wes had no problem with female members and neither did his friends. But the old guard still wasn't happy and usually fought the women on every change they tried to institute. Even something as stupid as what they were dealing with tonight—the color of the restrooms.

Wes focused on a trio of women across the room who were even now arguing with two older men whose faces were practically purple with suppressed rage. Shaking his head, Wes looked at his ex, Cecelia Morgan, and her pals Simone Parker and Naomi Price. The three of them together were surely annoying, but he'd always thought of them as benign, somehow. Now though, he had to wonder if the trio of Mean Girls were behind the Maverick business. Yet even as he thought it, Cecelia spouted off about the color of the walls in the women's restroom as if deciding on Springtime Peach was the most important thing in the world. Could she really be behind the devious attack on him?

While she propped her hands on her hips and

glared at the older man in the leather chair, Wes could hardly believe that once upon a time, he'd been involved with Cecelia. What the hell had he ever seen in her? Sure, she was gorgeous, but she and her friends still seemed to be locked into high-school behavior, living up to their nickname, the Mean Girls.

As he watched, Simone Parker, with her bold blue eyes, long black hair and body built to wake the dead, leaned into old man McGuire, shaking her finger in his face. Right beside her was stunning Naomi Price, with brown eyes and long reddish-brown hair. Naomi had a self-satisfied look on her face as she watched Simone battle with the old man. Cecelia, though, gave a glance around as if she were looking for a way out.

Briefly, her gaze met Wes's, and she must have read the disgust on his face, because damned if she didn't look embarrassed to be a part of the scene playing out in front of her. But thankfully, Cecelia was no longer Wes's problem.

As if he could read Wes's mind, Toby sighed and said, "Those three should have grown out of that nonsense after high school." He paused, then added, "Especially Naomi. That's just not who she is. Not really."

"I don't know," Tom put in. "The three of them have been bothering people in Royal for years. Maybe it's just become a habit for all of them."

"Then it's one they should break," Wes said, taking another sip of scotch.

"Agreed," Toby muttered darkly.

"All right now." Parker Reese, pediatrician at Royal Memorial hospital, spoke up loudly enough to be heard over everyone else. "Can we cut to the chase here? Let's get the decisions done so we can get out of here."

Normally, Parker was quiet, approachable, but not overly friendly. The crowd quieted, the club's president, Case Baxter, took over and the Mean Girls subsided into silence.

"Well, damn," Wes muttered. He might actually get out of this meeting in time to tuck Caroline in and read her a story. "It's a miracle."

"Yeah," Toby said, "I'm thinking we owe Parker a beer."

A couple hours later, he was home in bed, waiting for the woman he couldn't get enough of. When the bedroom door opened and Belle slipped inside, he smiled. "Caro asleep?"

"Out like a light," she said, "still clutching her doll to her chest. She hasn't come up with the right name for her yet, but she's working on it." Belle eased under the covers and moved in close to Wes, laying her head on his shoulder.

The big bed faced the fireplace, where a nice blaze was going, sending out flickering light and shadow around the room. He tucked his arm around her and held her close, thinking this just couldn't get much better.

A shame he had to shatter it. Holding on to her, just in case she tried to pull away, Wes said, "I spoke to a specialist in Houston today."

She stiffened in his arms, but only tipped her head back to look at him. "About…?"

Wes scowled. "You know what about. Caroline."

"Wes, we agreed that we'd decide on specialists *together*."

"I just talked to him, Belle," Wes said, stroking one hand up and down her back. "I didn't sign our girl up for surgery."

Seconds ticked past, and he watched as anger drained away to frustration, then to simple curiosity. "Okay, fine. What did he say?"

"That he couldn't tell me anything without examining Caro," Wes admitted, "which I knew already. I was just asking some general questions. To satisfy my own curiosity."

"And did you?"

"Yeah." He smoothed one hand through her hair, letting the silky tendrils slide through his fingers. "I wondered, what do you think about getting her a cochlear implant in only one ear?"

She frowned up at him and waited, so he continued.

"We could start out with one, let her go for a few years, see if there are more advancements made in the meantime, and then later on we can include her in the decision making. If she wants to get a second one, then we do that. If not, we don't."

He looked into her eyes and hoped she saw that he was only trying to figure out the best thing for Caroline. It wasn't easy to know what to do, and he figured all parents felt the same. Different issues, maybe, but no one had a game plan that would let them see the future. To *know* which path was the right one to take.

"When she's older, Caroline can tell us what she wants to do. But meanwhile, we make sure she doesn't lose too much ground."

Isabelle was quiet for so long, Wes half wondered if she'd just zoned out. But then she reached up and ran the tip of her finger across his lips. "You surprise me, Wes."

"Yeah?" He kissed her fingertip. "How?"

"That's an excellent compromise from a man not known for making them."

He gave her a wink. "I'm a great businessman. I know how to make deals that everyone can live with. Ask anyone."

"I don't have to ask." She gave him a wry smile. "I've seen you convince people to do things they had no intention of doing, and it looks like you've done it again."

"Yeah?" He smiled. Wes wasn't trying to fast-talk Belle into anything, but he couldn't pretend he wasn't going to do everything he could to help his child, either.

"Yeah," she repeated, and turned, bracing one arm across his chest as she looked at him. "I don't know why I didn't think of it myself. Somehow I convinced myself it was all or nothing, but it's not. We can ease into the implant situation and see how Caro responds."

"Exactly." Wes pulled her over to lie on top of

him and skimmed his hands down her back to her behind. She sighed and briefly closed her eyes before looking at him again, and he thought he'd never seen anything as beautiful as this woman.

"We can't get into the specialist until next week." He stared up into her eyes and watched as a layer of frost dazzled their surface. Belle never had been an easy woman, and he could see clearly that she was willing to dig her heels in.

"We won't be here next week," she said quietly.

"You could be. Stay." His hands gripped her hips to hold her in place, because he could tell she wanted to slide off him. Hard to argue with a man when you were both naked and pressed together. Which was exactly why he was keeping her right where she was.

"We've been through this already, Wes," she said. "Why should we stay?"

He watched those eyes of hers, felt himself drowning in them, and every instinct he possessed warned him to take a huge mental step back. To ease away. Let her slide off his body and put some distance between them. But he couldn't do it.

He knew he had to give her a reason to stay, and so he offered the only one he had. "I'm not ready for you to go."

She went still, her hands on his shoulders, her mouth no more than a breath away from his. He waited what felt like forever for her to speak. When she did, he released a breath he hadn't realized had been caught in his chest.

"Okay," she said softly. "We'll stay a few more days. To see the specialist."

A few more days wasn't forever, but it would do for now.

"Deal," he said, then rolled over, taking her with him, holding her body beneath his as he bent to take her nipple into his mouth.

She trembled and he felt like a damn king. She sighed and it was like music. Night after night, they came together, and it was always good. Always right. Always better than the time before. He couldn't get enough of her and didn't think he ever would.

Five long years without her had taught him that no other woman could compare to her. And he wasn't ready to lose her again just yet.

Her hands slid from his shoulders down his arms, and Wes felt every stroke like a line of fire dissolving into his bones. Sliding his hands along her body, he laid claim to her in the most intimate, ancient way. Every line and curve of her body became his as he tasted, touched, caressed.

Moonlight speared through the windows, bathing the room in a pale, silvery light. Her eyes caught that light, reflected it and shone like beacons, drawing Wes in closer, deeper. He felt himself falling and couldn't seem to stop it. Didn't know if he *wanted* to stop it.

At this moment, all he knew was that he needed to lose himself in the woman with him. She brought him confusion, laughter, warmth and the near constant need to be inside her. Wes ached for her night and day. The longer he was with her, the more that need intensified. That alone should have worried him, he knew. But the simple fact was, he didn't care what, if anything, it meant. All he could think about was *her.*

She arched into him, and Wes smiled against her skin. She moved against him, shifting her hips, letting him know that the ache inside was building. He loved that she felt what he did, that she wanted as desperately as he did. *Loved.* He blanked his mind at that wayward thought and gave himself up to the moment.

Wes skimmed one hand down to her core and cupped the heat nestled there. Instantly, she lifted her hips, rocking helplessly beneath his touch.

"Wes," she said on a sigh, "don't tease me..."

"Teasing's half the fun," he murmured and took first one nipple then the other into his mouth, tugging, suckling, relishing the tiny gasps and groans she made. He dipped one finger into her center, then another. He stroked her inside and out, while his thumb traced lazy, relentless circles over that most sensitive bud at the heart of her. She twisted in his grasp, moving her hips, arching her back, as her breath came faster, faster. He suckled at her breast, felt her tremble and knew it wasn't enough. He wanted her mindless, defenseless.

Sliding down the length of her body, he knelt between her thighs, scooped his hands beneath her bottom and raised her high off the mattress.

"Wes—" Her eyes were burning. Her hands fisted in the sheet beneath her as her legs dangled off the bed.

Keeping his gaze locked with hers, he bent his head to her center and covered her with his mouth. Instantly, her head tipped back into the bank of pillows behind her and her grip on the sheets tightened until her knuckles went white.

He smiled to himself as he used his lips, tongue and teeth to drive her to the brink, only to keep her from going over. He held her on the edge deliberately, feeling her shake and shiver, knowing what her body wanted, knowing how she craved it, because he did, too.

Again and again, his tongue laid claim to her and Wes knew he'd never hear anything more beautiful than the whimpering sighs sliding from her throat.

"Wes, please. Please."

He laid her down and reached for the bedside drawer. Grabbing a condom, he sheathed himself, then leaned over her to sheathe himself again…inside her. He entered her on a whisper, and she sighed at the sense of completion when he filled her. Wes closed his eyes and stayed perfectly still for a long moment, savoring the sensation of being held inside her body. The heat, the slick feel of her surrounding him. Then he opened his eyes, looked down into hers and murmured, "Enough."

"Now, Wes," she said, gripping his hips even as she lifted her legs to wrap them around him. *"Now."*

"Yes," he murmured and lowered his head to kiss her. His body rocked into hers, and he fell into a frantic rhythm, his hips pounding against hers, pushing them both faster, higher until release hung just within reach in the darkness. They lunged for it together and together they shattered, holding onto each other as they took the fall.

And with her wrapped in his arms, Wes closed his eyes and held her tight.

Nine

The following night, they left Caroline in Bobbi's care and went to dinner at the Texas Cattleman's Club. Isabelle had always loved the place, for its history, its meaning to the town of Royal. It had never bothered her that it had traditionally been an all-male private club. Heck, she figured women liked time to themselves, too. But now that women were welcome as members, she loved the changes that had only been started the last time she was in Royal.

There was a different feeling to the place. Not exactly feminine, but at least a few of the rough edges seemed to have been smoothed over.

"It's been a while since you've been here," Wes said, tucking her hand through the crook of his arm.

"Five years," she said, glancing up at him. He

looked gorgeous, of course, but then Wes Jackson would have to work at looking anything less than amazing. His black suit was elegantly tailored, and the deep red tie against the white dress shirt looked great. His hair was ruffled—she didn't suppose it would ever look anything but. And she liked it that way.

She was wearing a long-sleeved navy blue dress with a full skirt and a scooped neckline that just hinted at the cleavage beneath. Her black heels added three inches to her height, and she still had to look up to meet Wes's gaze. But she saw approval and desire in his eyes, so it was worth it. "Do you still come here for lunch every week?"

"Usually." He nodded to the waiter and headed for his favorite table. Wes seated Isabelle then sat down opposite her. "It's a good spot to get together and talk business."

Wine was served after a moment or two, and Isabelle's eyebrows arched. "Ordered ahead of time, did you? Think you know me that well?"

"Yes, I do." He leaned across the table and smiled. "Your favorite here is the chicken marsala and a side salad, blue cheese dressing."

"I don't know whether to be flattered that you remembered or appalled that I'm so predictable."

"Be flattered," he said. "You've never been predictable, Belle. You always did keep me guessing. Still do."

"I'm glad to know that," she said and took a sip of her wine. Setting the glass back down again, she looked at him, sitting there with all the quiet confidence of a king. He was in his element here, and she was on his turf. She'd have done well to remember that, but sadly, it was too late now. Isabelle had tumbled right back into love with the man, and there didn't seem to be a way out that didn't include a lot of pain.

"Thank you," he said, throwing her off balance again.

"For what?"

"For agreeing to stay into next week. To talk to the specialist with Caro."

They hadn't spoken about that since the night before, but then really, what was there to say? He'd caught her in a weak moment, Isabelle told herself. Naked and wrapped up in his arms, she might have agreed to anything. So she could hardly be blamed for putting off leaving for a few more days. Besides, Caroline loved it here.

Her little girl spent hours in the stable with the head groom, Davey. He was teaching her about horses and had already taught her how to brush her pony, Sid, named after her favorite character in the *Ice Age* movies, and feed him. Caroline was thriving, with both of her parents at her side, with Bobbi and Tony. Not to mention Robin and everyone at the Houston office.

She was a sweet girl and people responded to that, making Caroline feel like a princess wherever she went. In fact, Caro hadn't once asked about going home. Which should, Isabelle thought, worry her. When they did eventually leave, it would be a hard thing for Caroline. It was going to be nearly impossible for Isabelle.

"You're welcome," she said, shoving those dark thoughts down into a corner of her mind. "I'm interested in what the specialist has to say, too."

"Good." He lifted his glass, looked past her and sighed. "Damn it."

"What is it?" She made to turn around, but he stopped her.

"Don't look. It's Cecelia Morgan, and it looks like she's coming over here."

Wes's ex-girlfriend. When she was in Royal before, Isabelle and Cecelia had been friendly, but never friends. The last time she'd spoken to Cecelia, the woman had happened upon her while Isabelle was indulging in a good cry. After hearing her out, Cecelia had urged Isabelle to leave Royal, insisting that Wes would never be interested in a child or commitment or any of the other things that Isabelle had wanted so badly.

"Hi, Wes," the woman said with a cautious smile as she stopped at their table. "Isabelle."

"Hello, Cecelia," Isabelle said, wondering why the woman looked so uncomfortable. "It's nice to see you again."

The other woman smiled wryly, clearly not believing the platitude.

Cecelia was beautiful, with her blond hair, long legs and a figure that would make most women incredibly jealous. But right now her green eyes were filled with regret that had Isabelle curious.

"Look," Cecelia said softly, giving a quick look around the room to make sure she wasn't being overheard. "I don't mean to interrupt, so I won't be long. I just had to stop and say something to both of you."

"What is it, Cecelia?" Wes asked, his deep, curt voice anything but welcoming.

The other woman heard the ice in his voice and stiffened in response. "I just wanted to apologize to you. Both of you. I should have told you about your daughter, Wes. And Isabelle, I never should have said that Wes wouldn't want his child. I feel terrible for my part in all of this and I just wanted to say I'm really sorry."

"Cecelia—I don't blame you for that." Isabelle reached out to her, but the other woman shook her head and held up one hand for quiet.

"It's okay. I just saw you both here and I wanted to say that I've got some regrets over things I did in the past. That's all." She took a step back. "So, just… enjoy your dinner." And she was gone.

"That was weird," Wes said. "I don't think I've ever seen her so thoughtful."

"It was unexpected," Isabelle agreed. She wouldn't have believed that Cecelia would ever apologize like that. The woman had never been concerned with anyone beyond herself and her two best friends. But maybe, Isabelle thought, as her gaze settled on Wes, people really could change.

The next morning, Wes was at the Houston office for a few hours before heading home to take Belle and Caroline to a park. He laughed to himself at the thought. Hell, even with the upcoming launch, he'd taken more time off lately than he had in years. And though he'd never been one to delegate important duties, he'd been doing just that more and more lately—and feeling his priorities shift as if they'd taken on a life of their own. Business had always been his joy. His passion. Growing his companies had been the focus of his life—until he'd discovered he was a father. One little girl—and her mother—had changed everything for Wes.

He leaned back in his desk chair and stared out the window at the steel-gray winter sky. January in Texas didn't mean snow like Colorado, but the weather could change on a dime and usually did. The park might not be the best destination for today.

"Boss?"

He turned his head to Robin in the open doorway. "What is it?"

"You're not going to believe this," she said, worrying her bottom lip, "but Teddy Bradford is on video call for you."

Frowning, Wes straightened up. Teddy hadn't taken Wes's calls since all of this started. Granted, Wes had been focused more on damage control than in trying to reach out to Teddy—especially after the press conference the man had held. Still, the CEO of PlayCo had been silent up until now, so what had changed?

"Put him through." Wes turned to the monitor on

his desk and waited. Teddy's face appeared on the screen moments later.

The older man was in his sixties, with salt-and-pepper hair and shrewd green eyes. He was in good shape and in person was an imposing figure. But Wes wasn't so easily intimidated.

"Bradford," he said, with a nod of greeting.

"Jackson." Teddy gave him a benevolent smile and folded his hands together, laying the tips of his index fingers against his chin. "I thought it was time we talked."

"Why now?" Best to play his cards close to the vest. Wes had learned early on when people were caught up in casual conversation, they made slips. So he watched what he said and tried to make the other man give away his secrets instead.

Teddy leaned back in his oversize maroon leather chair. "I've seen the pictures of you with your daughter and her mother. You're making quite the splash, publicity-wise."

Understanding dawned. Hell, this was just what Wes had originally hoped for. He'd known that photographers would be following him around hoping to get more dirt to feed the scandal that had erupted almost two weeks ago. Instead, the pictures were of him, Belle and Caro together. Happy. Enjoying each other. And he had known that people would assume they were the family they appeared to be.

The plan had worked great. Except that Wes no longer felt as if he were pretending. Things had changed for him, he realized. It wasn't a subterfuge anymore. The situation felt real to him, and he couldn't imagine living without Belle and Caro. That was an unsettling thought for a man who'd spent his entire life avoiding commitment, love and any semblance of family.

Putting all of that aside for the moment, he asked, "Why exactly are you calling, Teddy?"

The older man's face creased in an avuncular smile that instantly rubbed Wes the wrong way.

"That takeover could be back on the table for you," Teddy said, dropping his hands to rest on his desktop. "As a family man myself, I can appreciate when a man makes a mistake and sets it right. You getting things straight with the mother of your child has made me look at you in a new light."

Pompous old bastard. What Wes really wanted to do was hang up. Teddy Bradford as the arbiter of family values was annoying enough. Knowing that he had somehow gotten the old goat's approval really stuck in his craw.

"You should know, though," Teddy continued, in that oh-so-confidential tone, "that we've had another offer for the company. I wanted to give you a heads-up before I make any decisions. Maybe we can still work something out on the merger."

Wes's expression didn't give away what he was thinking. Mainly because he wasn't sure how he felt about any of this. Taking over PlayCo, blending it into his own company had been his purpose for a couple of years now. A part of him was eager at the chance to seal the very deal that had been shattered so completely by the mysterious Maverick. Yet there was another part of Wes that was standing back, wary of this sudden magnanimous burst from the other man.

"Shame about that little gal of yours," Teddy was saying with a sad shake of his head. "Saw she's got a set of hearing aids. Looks like she'll have some challenges ahead."

Wes gritted his teeth. Caroline was the most amazing kid he'd ever met. Hearing or not, she was way better than this man's version of *challenged.*

"I appreciate the phone call," Wes said, somehow managing to hide the guilt nearly choking him. "But like you said in that press conference, I've got a lot of thinking to do."

"Is that right?"

"Teddy," Wes said, "there's a lot going on right now, so I'll have to get back to you on this."

"See that you do," Teddy said, then stabbed a finger at the disconnect button and the screen went dark.

For a second or two, Wes just sat at his desk as fury ebbed and flowed inside him. At Bradford. At the situation he'd found himself in. At himself for dragging Belle and Caro into this mess. The merger with PlayCo was huge. He was being offered the very merger he'd been working toward for two years. But taking it, he might have to swallow more than he was willing to. And Wes didn't know if he could do it. Or even if he was interested in trying.

Still, there was more to think about here than

just himself. Expanding the company meant hiring more people, and that was good for everyone. And hadn't this been exactly what he'd been aiming for all along? So what was he waiting for? Why was he easing back from the very thing he'd been counting on?

He scrubbed both hands over his face. "Robin!"

Seconds later, his assistant appeared in the doorway.

"Gather the heads of every department," he said. "I want them here in an hour, discussing that call from Bradford."

"Yes, boss."

When she left, Wes was alone with his thoughts again. And he didn't much like them.

Isabelle stopped by the Royal Diner to pick up the lunch she'd ordered. Amanda Battle, the diner's owner, was at the counter, waiting with Isabelle's takeout bag. Inside that bag were Wes's favorites—grilled ham-and-cheese sandwiches and fresh onion rings. Not the healthiest lunch in the world, Isabelle thought, but a spontaneous office picnic required more than raw veggies and a salad.

Wes was supposed to come home early and take her and Caro out for the afternoon. But Isabelle had received such great news from home, she hadn't wanted to wait to see him. So an office picnic sounded like fun. Besides, Wes had been devoting so much time to her and Caro, Isabelle knew he had a lot of work to catch up on. The new toy launch was still a few weeks away, but he had to be on-site to handle any problems that might crop up.

She couldn't wait to tell him that the toys she'd selected from Wes's company had already arrived in Swan Hollow. And they'd sent so much more than she'd expected, Isabelle was sure she could supply two or three children's wards with those toys alone.

But as good as the news was, it also meant she had to leave for home soon. The distribution of toys was always a logistical nightmare, and she had to be there to supervise it all. She hated the thought of leaving, which was silly since that had been the plan all along. But things had changed, hadn't they? Wes had changed. So maybe after the work was done in Swan Hollow, she and Caro could come back. Maybe.

"Well, it's about time you came in to see me."

Isabelle cleared her mind, slid onto one of the counter stools and smiled at Amanda. "Sorry, I've been busy."

"So I heard." Amanda slid a cup of coffee toward her. "In fact, the whole town's been talking about you and Wes and your daughter almost nonstop. And you know the diner is the unofficial clearinghouse for information."

Isabelle winced, knowing that she was the subject of gossip and speculation. But honestly, she'd expected nothing less. Royal's lifeblood was gossip, and if you wanted to find out the latest news, you came to the Royal Diner.

"Bobbi had your daughter in here yesterday for a milkshake," Amanda said. "She's a cutie."

"Thanks." Isabelle glanced around the familiar diner and was glad to see it hadn't changed. Black-and-white floors, red vinyl booths, and the delicious scent of cheeseburgers cooking on the grill. She was also happy to see there weren't many customers this early in the day.

"How's Wes taking being an instant daddy?" Amanda asked, leaning against the counter.

Back when Isabelle was living in Texas, she'd spent a lot of time in Royal. She and Amanda had become friends, and it was really good to see her again. Actually, she'd enjoyed a lot about being back in Royal and hadn't really expected to, since she'd left Texas so abruptly, thinking to put it all behind her.

"It's been a little iffy," Isabelle said honestly. "He's crazy about Caroline and the feeling's mutual."

"But…?"

She smiled and sighed. Amanda always had been too intuitive. "But I have the same problem I did five years ago," she admitted. "I love him and he likes me. And just how fifth grade does that sound?" She sighed and gave in to her inner worries. "I just don't know if this is going to work or not."

"Sweetie," Amanda said softly, "nobody ever knows that going in. With Nathan and I, it was touch and go from the beginning. But it was worth it. So don't give up. Just ride it out and hope for the best."

Good advice, she thought, and if it was just *her*, maybe she would. But she had Caroline to worry about now, too. And she couldn't justify risking her little girl's heart on the off chance that Wes would see how good they all were together and want it to be permanent.

Although… "Wes has been…different," Isabelle said, keeping her voice low, confidential, just in case there were any big ears listening in. "He's warmer than he was. More reachable somehow. Less obsessed with his business. Sometimes I look at him and I think, it could work. And then I worry that I'm seeing what I want to see. Basically," she said on a choked laugh, "I'm going a little crazy."

Amanda laughed and patted her hand. "Isabelle, we're *all* a little crazy."

Smiling ruefully, she admitted, "I hate that I'm getting pulled in, but Amanda, I keep thinking that this time Wes and I might have the chance to build something."

Amanda sighed in commiseration. "Sweetie, if he has a brain in his head, he won't mess this up."

"I hope you're right."

When Isabelle reached the office in Houston, Robin wasn't at her desk, but the door to Wes's inner sanctum was partially open. Thinking he and Robin were going over some work, she approached quietly and listened, not wanting to interrupt.

"It worked perfectly." A man's voice spoke up. "Bradford was so impressed seeing pictures of you, Isabelle and Caroline together, he's giving you everything you wanted."

Isabelle took a breath and held it as she stood, rooted to the spot.

Another man spoke up. "Maybe Maverick did you a favor, bringing this all out into the open."

Isabelle sucked in a breath.

"Maverick, whoever he or she is, wasn't trying to help me. And I still want the IT department working on finding out just who the hell he or she is."

"Right. Sorry, boss."

Isabelle's throat was tight and her stomach was alive with nerves.

"Back to Bradford," Wes said. "He's still talking about another offer on the table."

"Yes," a woman answered, "but he called you. Clearly he prefers selling out to us."

The man spoke up again, and Isabelle was pretty sure she recognized the voice as Mike from the PR department. "If you can just make the whole family thing work for another couple of weeks, we could seal the deal."

Family thing. Had it all been an act? A performance for Teddy Bradford? Had any of what she'd felt in the last week or more been real?

"I'm not waiting two weeks to give Bradford my decision," Wes said.

Heart dropping to her feet, Isabelle backed away from the door. No, she told herself. Nothing was real. It was all for show. All to help Wes nail down the merger that was, in spite of what she'd believed, still all important to him. Clutching the takeout bag, she bumped into the edge of Robin's desk and staggered. She felt as though the world was tipping beneath her feet. Everything she'd thought, hoped for, was a lie. How could she have been so stupid?

Wes had only been using her and Caroline to fight back against that Twitter attack and the crashing of his business plans. How could she have believed even for a second that he'd meant any of it? That he'd suddenly learned how to love?

Furious with him but even more with herself, Isabelle turned to leave, then stopped at Robin's voice. "Oh, hi, Isabelle. Are you here to see the boss?"

Panicked, desperate to escape, she forced a smile and shook her head. "It's not important. He's busy. Here." She handed the bag of food to the other woman and left, this time at a sprint.

Robin came back into the office carrying a Royal Diner takeout bag, and Wes frowned. "You called in for takeout from *Royal*?"

"Nope," she said. "Isabelle was in the outer office. She brought this for you, but she left because she could see you're busy."

Busy. Wes's brain raced, going back over everything that had been said in the last few minutes. Had Isabelle heard it? Was that why she left? *Damn it.* He jumped up from behind his desk and hit the door at a dead run. "I'll be back."

He didn't bother with the elevator—it would have taken too long. Why the hell had she chosen *today* to surprise him? If she'd heard any of what was being said in his office, she had to be furious. But she'd calm down once he explained. He bolted down the stairs and hit the parking garage just as the elevator arrived and Isabelle stepped out. She took one look at him and her features iced over.

Explaining wasn't going to be as easy as he'd hoped. "Belle—"

"Don't." She hurried past him. "I don't want to talk to you right now."

He took hold of her upper arm and didn't let go when her gaze shifted meaningfully to his hand on her. The parking garage was cold, dark, and their voices were echoing through the structure. Overhead lights fought the darkness and squares of watery sunlight speared in through the entrance and exits.

"Damn it, you don't understand."

"I understand everything," she countered, yanking her arm free. "Maverick messed up your plans."

"Damn right he did."

"And everything with me, with Caro, was all a lie. You *used* us to get that stupid merger that's so important to you."

Insulted, mostly because her accusation held a hell of a lot of truth, Wes swallowed his own anger before speaking again. "That merger was important. Something I've been working toward for years. But I wasn't using you. Either of you."

"Sure." She nodded sharply, her eyes narrowed on him. "I believe you."

"Yeah, I can see that." Helplessness rose up in him and nearly choked his air off. Wes hated this feeling and could honestly say that until he'd met Isabelle, he'd never really experienced it. "I don't know what you heard—"

She sneered at him. "I heard all I needed to."

He thought back fast, recalling what everyone was saying in the minutes before he'd found out she'd run off. Gritting his teeth at the memory, he said, "It was out of context."

"Right."

His anger burst free. "Are you going to listen to me about this or just keep agreeing with me to shut me up?"

"Which will get me out of here the fastest?" She folded her arms over her chest and tapped the toe of her shoe against the concrete in a staccato beat.

Irritating, fascinating, infuriating woman.

Scowling, he said, "Did it hurt that pictures of the three of us were in the news? No. But did I arrange it? No. I didn't lie to you, Belle."

"Really." She tipped her head to one side. "Explain Caro's bedroom."

"What?"

"Murals on the wall. Rugs. Chairs. New bed. Toys." She ticked them all off, then said, "You started preparing for our arrival long before you asked me to come to Texas. This was all a plan from the beginning."

"Yeah," he said, refusing to deny this much, at least. "When I found out I had a daughter—after her mother had lied to me about it for five years—I had a room set up for her. That makes me a bad guy?"

She shook her head. "You don't get it. But then, you never did." She started walking again.

"What the hell? You don't finish an argument? You just walk off."

"This argument *is* finished," she called back, and the click of her heels on concrete sounded out like beats of a drum.

He let her go. No point chasing her down to keep arguing here. He'd give her time to calm down. Let her get back home, think everything through.

Wes listened to her car door slam and the engine fire up. "Once she settles a bit, it'll be fine," he told himself. "I'll fix all of it tonight."

Ten

Belle wasn't there when he got home.

At first, he couldn't believe it. He'd expected to find her in the great room, quietly stewing. Wes had arrived, flowers in hand, ready to smooth out every rut between them and charm her into seeing things his way. The reasonable way.

Now, he stood in the empty room, a bouquet of lavender peonies gripped in one tight fist. There was no sign of either his wife or his daughter.

Wife?

That word had popped into his head from God knew where, and Wes rubbed his forehead as if trying to erase it. But it wouldn't go. When had he started thinking of Belle as a wife? About the time, he figured, that he'd realized he had no interest in living his life without the two people who meant everything to him. Staggered, he shook his head and kept looking around the room.

None of Caroline's toys were lying abandoned in the middle of the floor. Belle's electronic tablet wasn't on the coffee table, and the house *felt* empty.

His heart fisted in his chest, and a soul-deep ache settled over him. Why the hell would she leave? He pushed one hand through his hair and turned a fast circle, checking every damn corner of the empty room as if somehow expecting Isabelle and Caroline to simply appear out of thin air. "She was supposed to *be* here," he muttered. "We're supposed to straighten this out. She's supposed to *listen* to me, damn it."

Refusing to believe that she would simply leave without a word, without even a damn note, he headed for the stairs and was stopped halfway across the hall.

"They're gone."

He stared at Bobbi and ground out, "When?"

"A few hours ago." She leaned one shoulder against the doorjamb and crossed her arms over her chest.

Hours? They'd left hours ago?

"Why the hell didn't you call me at work?" he demanded. "Let me know?"

"Because she asked me not to," Bobbi snapped, her gaze drilling into his.

Looked like Belle wasn't the only woman he'd pissed off today. His housekeeper was clearly disgusted with him. But that didn't excuse her keeping this from him.

"You realize that you don't work for Belle, right?"

"And you realize that I'm on her side in this, right?"

When had he lost complete control of his world? This kind of thing just didn't happen to Wes Jackson. "You're fired," he said tightly.

"No, I'm not," she retorted and pushed off the wall. Wagging one finger at him, she added, "You can't fire me, because you *need* me. Just like you need Isabelle and your daughter."

He felt the punch of those words as he would have a fist. She was right. He was alone and she was right. He did need them. Wes scowled more fiercely, not knowing whom he was more angry with. Bobbi? Or himself?

"That little girl was *crying* when they left."

Himself, he thought. He was definitely most angry at himself. And yet, Belle hadn't had to leave. She should have stayed. Talked this out. Wes swallowed back a fresh tide of anger rising up from the pit of his belly. Sure, he'd screwed up. But Belle had walked out. Caro had been crying. Had Belle cried, too? Regret shattered the anger, and guilt buried what was left. So many emotions were charging around inside him, it was a wonder Wes could draw a breath at all.

"You should have called me." Turning his back on Bobbi, he took the stairs three at a time and headed straight to the master bedroom.

No sign of Belle there, either. Somehow, he'd

wanted to believe that his housekeeper had been lying to him. That she was trying to make him wise up before facing Isabelle. But she hadn't lied. He threw the walk-in closet door open and stared at the empty rack where Belle's clothes had been hanging only that morning.

Hell, her scent was still there, lingering in the still air. Haunting him until her face rose up in his mind and he couldn't see anything else. But she was gone.

He left his bedroom, stalked across the hall to Caro's room and felt his heart rip when he found it as empty as the rest of the house. A soft whining sound caught his ear and he looked around the door to the child-size couch. Abbey was stretched out, as if waiting for Caro to come back. The dog lifted her head when he entered, then seeing him alone, whined again and dropped her head to her paws.

Wes knew just how she felt.

He glanced down at the peonies he still held in his clenched fist. Then he dropped them to the floor and stepped on the fragile petals on the way out of the room.

Grabbing his cell phone, Wes walked across his bedroom until he was staring out over the yard. He hit speed dial, and while he waited, he looked at the stables, then the corral, where Caro's pony was wandering alone. His daughter should be there right now. Waving at him. Signing to him. But no, her mother had taken her away. *Again.*

He was so wrapped up in his own thoughts, it

startled him when a voice came on the line and said, "She doesn't want to speak to you."

"What?" Wes yanked the phone from his ear and glanced at the number he'd dialed, making sure it was Belle's. But there was no mistake.

"Edna?" he asked, realizing Belle's housekeeper was running interference for her. She couldn't even talk to him on the *phone*? "Where's Belle?"

"She's here at home where she belongs," Belle's housekeeper informed him. "And she asked me to tell you she's got nothing more to say to you. She says that everything that needed saying was said this morning."

He held the phone so tight, it should have shattered in his grasp. Taking one long, deep breath, Wes reached down deep for patience and came up empty-handed. He couldn't believe that she was going to such lengths to avoid him.

"So her answer is to run away?" he countered.

"She didn't run. She flew."

Was he paying off some terrible karma from a past life? Why else would every woman he knew be giving him such a hard time? Couldn't they all see that there were two sides to this?

"Damn it, Edna, put her on the phone."

"Don't you curse at me. And I don't take orders from you."

He was beginning to wonder if *anyone* did. Taking another deep breath, he held it for a second, then released it to calmly ask, "Can I speak to my daughter then?"

"Nope."

A fresh rush of anger surged through him at the nonchalant attitude. He'd never been more frustrated in his life. Separated from his family by hundreds of miles and an emotional chasm that appeared too deep to cross. "You can't keep her from me."

"I can't, no," she said flatly. "But Isabelle can, and good for her, I say. You had a chance at something wonderful and you threw it away. You threw *them* away. I know what you did, so if you're looking for understanding, you dialed the wrong damn number."

Then she hung up.

Stunned, Wes stared at his phone for a long second. *Nobody* hung up on him! "What the hell is wrong with everybody?"

There was no answer to his strangled question. His cell didn't ring; the blank screen taunted him. So he threw his window open, pitched the phone into the yard, then slammed the sash down again.

And he still didn't feel better.

"What did he say?" Isabelle looked at Edna.

"I think it's fair to say that his cookies are completely frosted." Handing the phone back, Edna picked up a plate of brownies and set it in front of Isabelle. "He's mad, of course, and I think a little hurt."

"I doubt it." Edna was too nice, too optimistic. Wes wasn't hurt—just frustrated that she hadn't fallen in line with his plan. You couldn't hurt Wes Jackson with a sledgehammer. A person had to *care* to be hurt.

Like her daughter cared. Just as Isabelle had feared, leaving Texas had been a misery for Caroline. The drama from earlier that day was still playing through her mind.

"But I don't want to go," the little girl had wailed, bottom lip jutting out in a warning sign of a meltdown approaching.

"I know you don't," Isabelle told her. "But it's time we left. We have things to do at home, baby girl."

She sniffled dramatically. "Like what?"

"School."

"I can go to school here. Wes says so."

Oh, thanks so much for that, Isabelle thought with a new burst of anger at the infuriating man. "You already have a school. And Edna and Marco and your uncles miss us."

"But I will miss Wes. And Abbey! Abbey sleeps with me, Mommy. She'll be sad if I go away."

Isabelle sighed. "The dog is not supposed to be sleeping in your bed."

"We sleep on my couch."

"Perfect," she muttered and threw the rest of Caro's clothes into the suitcase. A cab would be there to pick them up in twenty minutes, and the charter jet was waiting on the tarmac. Sometimes, she thought, it was good to be rich. At least she didn't have to wait for a commercial flight and chance having to deal with Wes again. "Go get your doll, sweetie."

"I don't want to leave Wes. And Abbey. And Tony. And Bobbi. And Sid."

Isabelle sighed. She hated putting Caro through

this. Hated even more that it was all her fault for coming to Texas in the first place. For risking so much. For wanting to believe that she and Wes could share a future as well as a past. She should have known better. But apparently, one heartbreak in a lifetime just wasn't enough for her.

"Mommy, I don't wanna go!" Hands were flying and Isabelle wondered how her daughter managed to shout in sign language.

"We have to go." My God, Isabelle could actually feel her patience dissolving. She understood what Caro felt, but there was nothing she could do to ease any of it. The best thing for all of them was to leave Texas as quickly as possible. Get back to normal. So she stooped to what all parents eventually surrendered to. Bribery. "When we get home, we'll get you the puppy you wanted, okay?"

Caro's little hands flashed like mad as her features twisted and her eyes narrowed. "Don't want another dog. Want Abbey."

Things had not improved from there. Caro had cried and pleaded and begged, then at last had resorted to not speaking to her mother at all. By that point, Isabelle had been grateful for the respite. But she knew that tomorrow morning when her darling daughter woke up, there was still going to be trouble.

"God, I'm an idiot," she muttered and sipped at the tea Edna had made for her. Not only was her daughter miserable, but Isabelle's own heart was breaking. How could she have been so stupid to love Wes again? To hope again?

"Oh, honey, you're in love," Edna said with a wave of her hand. "That makes idiots of all of us."

She lifted her gaze to the other woman. "I never should have let Caro's heart get involved. How could I have done that to my daughter?"

"She's *his* daughter, too, honey." Sighing, Edna added, "I know you don't want to hear it right now, but the fact is, he has a right to know her and a right for Caro to know him."

Disgusted with herself, Isabelle muttered, "Well, if you're going to use logic..."

Laughing now, her old friend said, "Take the tea up to your room. A couple brownies wouldn't hurt, either. Get a good night's sleep. There'll be plenty of time tomorrow to worry yourself sick over all this."

"Maybe I will," Isabelle said and stood up. She'd go to her room, but she knew she wouldn't be sleeping. Instead, she'd be lying awake, remembering the last time she'd seen Wes and the flicker of guilt she'd read in his eyes.

"Where the hell did it all go sideways?" he asked the empty room and then actually paused to see if the universe would provide an answer.

But there was nothing. Just his own circling thoughts and the relentless silence in the house. He'd never minded it before. Hell, he'd relished it. Having this big place all to himself—but for Bobbi—had been like an island of peace.

Now it was more like a prison.

And he paced the confines of it all night as any

good prisoner should. He went from room to room, staring out windows, listening to his own footsteps on the wood floor. He let Abbey out and stood in the cold January night, tipping his head back to look at the ink-black sky with the bright pinpoints of stars glittering down at him. Then he and the dog, who was yet another female ignoring him, went back into the house and were stuck with each other.

And in the quiet, Wes remembered the meeting that morning. Remembered everyone talking about the merger and how the pictures of him and his family had saved the situation with PlayCo. Recalled that even he had talked about it.

Mostly though, he remembered the look on Belle's face when he caught up with her in the parking garage. The hurt. The betrayal. He took a breath, looked around his empty bedroom and knew what he had to do. Dawn was just streaking the sky when he picked up the phone.

"More news out of Texas this morning," the stock reporter on the TV said. "Renewed talks of a merger between Texas Toy Goods Inc. and PlayCo have ended. Again." The reporter smiled, checked her notes and continued. "This time though, it's Wes Jackson, CEO of Texas Toy Goods, who's backing away. Mr. Jackson confirmed the news earlier today. So far, Teddy Bradford hasn't been available for a comment."

Isabelle stared at the television as if she couldn't

believe what she'd just heard. "Why would he do that? Why would he call off the merger?"

Chance stood in the middle of the room and shrugged. "Maybe he finally realized there are other things more important."

She looked at her oldest brother and wondered. About this time yesterday, she'd walked into Wes's office for a surprise picnic only to have the world fall out from beneath her feet. Now, it felt like it was happening all over again. What was she supposed to think? Why did he stop a merger that he'd been so determined to pull off? Did he expect her to see that report and come running back to him? Oh, God, what did it say about her that she *wanted* to?

The doorbell rang, and since Chance was up already, he said, "I'll get it. You stay here."

Her brothers had circled the wagons as soon as she came home. While Chance kept her company, Eli and Tyler were with Caro in the kitchen while she had lunch. It was good to have family. Especially when everything seemed to be going so wrong.

"Okay, thanks," she said, curling up on the couch to watch the financial reports, hoping for more of a clue as to what Wes was up to.

When she heard the argument from the front hallway, though, Isabelle jolted to her feet, one hand slapped to her chest, as though she could soothe her suddenly galloping heart. Two voices, raised.

"What're you doing here?" Chance demanded.

"I'm here to see Belle. And my daughter."

Wes's voice. Hard. Implacable. Her heart jumped

again, and the pit of her stomach came alive with what felt like thousands of butterflies. She couldn't believe he was here. He'd come to her. Why? Isabelle turned to the doorway and stood completely still. Waiting.

"Get out of my way, Chance," Wes grumbled.

"I warned you once what would happen to you if you made either my sister or my niece cry."

"Don't try to stop me."

"You don't deserve them, you know."

"You're probably right," Wes said. "But they're my family and no one can keep me from them."

For a moment, Isabelle held her breath, shocked to the bone by what Wes had said.

"Don't blow this again," Chance warned.

A moment or two later, Wes was there, staring at her, and what she saw in his eyes stunned her. He'd always been so locked down. So emotionally distant that he was practically unreadable. But today, everything she'd ever dreamed of seeing was there, in his beautiful sea-green eyes.

Drawn by the loud argument, Eli and Tyler marched into the room, too, and Isabelle's three brothers formed a half circle behind Wes. Supportive? Threatening? She couldn't be sure, and at the moment, she didn't care. All she could see was Wes and all she felt was a rising sense of hope that fluttered to life in the center of her chest.

Wes didn't care about her brothers, either. He'd known before he arrived that he'd have to force his way past the Graystone wall of protection, and he'd been prepared for it. The brothers had given him a welcome as icy as the Colorado weather, but it didn't matter. He'd been willing to face anything to reach Isabelle.

Looking at her now, his heart thrummed in his chest and he took his first easy breath since the night before, when he'd found her gone and the world as he'd known it had ended. He crossed the room to her in a few long strides and stopped when he was within touching distance. God, he wanted to reach out to her, but there were things he had to say first. Things she needed to hear. Ignoring her brothers, he focused on the only woman he'd ever loved and started talking.

"I was wrong."

She blinked at him, and he read the surprise on her face.

Smiling sadly, he went on in a rush. "I know. I don't say that often. But I was stupid. Shortsighted. Stubborn. I never should have let you leave me five years ago. And I can't let you go now."

"Wes—"

"No," he said, quickly interrupting her. "Let me say this, Belle. Say what's needed saying for way too long."

She nodded, and he felt a wild flicker of optimism in his chest. He couldn't stop looking at her. Her beautiful eyes were wide with a mixture of disbelief and expectation. Her blond hair fell loose to her shoulders and the blue sweater she wore over jeans made her eyes look deeper, as if they held every secret in the universe.

Shaking his head, he began, "See, when my mother died, my father lived the rest of his life in misery. He never recovered, because he'd loved her too much." He reached out, laid both hands on her shoulders and smiled because he was there, with her again. This was the most important speech he'd ever make and he hoped to hell he'd find the right words. "I promised myself I'd never let a woman mean that much to me. It was a kid's reaction. A kid's vow—and it guided me most of my life. Yesterday though, I realized that I had never looked beyond my Dad's pain. But now I see that the happiness my father had before he lost my mom was worth the risk. Worth everything."

God, it sounded pitiful, even to him. He'd lived his life in fear. Love had had him running for years. And he'd never realized that by evading it, he'd been missing out on the best part of life. Well, no more.

"I love you, Isabelle," he said. "I loved you five years ago. I love you now. I will always love you."

She took a breath and swayed slightly in place, lifting one hand to her mouth. Absently, Wes heard her brothers leave the room, and he was grateful. He wanted privacy for this. For the most important moment of his life.

"I want to believe," she said, and he could see the truth of that in her eyes. "But how can I risk Caro's heart? She was devastated when we left yesterday. She cried herself to sleep last night."

He closed his eyes briefly and silently cursed. If he hadn't been so stupid, he never would have hurt his child. Hurt the woman he loved. Created such a damn mess out of everything.

"It tears at me to hear that," he said. "But you can trust me, Belle." He looked into her eyes and willed her to see the truth. "You'll never be rid of me again. Even if you tell me to go away today, I'll just come back. I'll keep trying for however long it takes to convince you that you're all I want. All I need."

She bit her bottom lip, and tears welled in her eyes. Feeling hope lift like a helium balloon in his chest, Wes kept talking. "I called off the merger."

"I know. I saw it on the news. I couldn't believe it."

"Yes, you can. I put Teddy off. None of that matters to me anymore. The only merger I'm interested in is the one between us. Marry me, Belle. You and Caroline come home with me. Build a future and a family with me."

"Oh, Wes..."

He smiled now, because he could see that she believed. That she was going to say yes. "You can design toys for the company, and together, we'll make sure Caro's Toybox is big enough that every child around the world has a toy to play with and a stuffed animal to cuddle."

A short, choked laugh shot from her throat.

Now that he was on a roll, he just kept building on the future he could see so clearly. "I want more kids, Belle. Brothers, sisters for Caroline. I want us to build a family so strong, not even your hardheaded brothers could tear it down."

She laughed again, louder this time, and reached up to cup his face between her palms. He closed his eyes briefly and released the last of his worries. The heat of her touch sank into him, reaching down into the darkest, loneliest corners of his heart, and left him breathless.

"It's not my brothers you have to worry about, Wes," she said, with a slow shake of her head. "It's *me*. Because once I say yes, I'm never letting you go."

Wes grinned. "That is the best news I've ever heard. So are you saying yes?"

"How could I not? I love you, Wes. I always have. So yes, I'll marry you and have babies with you and build a future filled with family."

"Thank God," he whispered, then reached into his pocket. Showing her the small blue velvet box, he opened it to reveal a square-cut emerald surrounded by diamonds.

"It's beautiful," she whispered.

He slid it onto her finger. "*Now* it's beautiful."

Then he kissed her, and she melted against him while Wes gave silent thanks for whatever gods had blessed him with a second chance at the love of a lifetime.

"Hey, you two," Eli called out. "Come up for air. There's a little girl here who wants to say hi."

They broke apart, and Wes looked down into the shining face of his daughter. Caro was staring up at him with pleasure in her eyes and a delighted smile on her face. She wore the red plastic heart that had first started him out on the journey that had led him here to this amazing moment. Shooting a quick look at Belle, he grinned. "I can't believe you saved that necklace."

Her smile was soft, tender. "It was the first thing you ever gave me. And Caro loves it. She loves you too, Wes. It's time she knows who you are."

Nodding, Wes went down on one knee in front of his daughter. Weirdly, nerves rattled the pit of his stomach. "I missed you," he said and signed.

"Me too," she answered, then threw her arms around his neck.

The force of that hug freely given shook Wes to his soul. Tears burned his eyes, so he closed them, reveling in the knowledge that he would never lose Belle and his daughter again. Then he pulled back, looked into her eyes and said softly, "I'm your father, Caro, and I love you very much."

Her eyes went wide and her mouth dropped open. She shifted her gaze to her mother and asked, "Really?"

"Really, baby," Belle said through her tears.

The little girl looked at Wes again and gave him a bright, happy smile. Her fingers flying along with the words pouring from her, she asked, "You're my daddy?"

"Yes," Wes said and signed.

"I wished that you were," she said, grinning now. "And my wish came true! I love you, Wes. I mean, *Daddy*."

His heart burst in a sweet blast of love and joy as Wes reached out to scoop her up and stand, still holding her close. Balancing his daughter on one arm he draped the other around Belle's shoulders and knew he'd never been more complete.

Completely shattered still as his daughter's simple words made him feel like the luckiest man on the face of the planet, he paid no attention to Belle's grinning brothers, still watching. He simply handed Caroline to her mother to free his hands and then he carefully signed, "I love you, too, baby girl."

Caroline clapped, Belle laughed and sighed all at once, and the Graystone brothers were applauding.

Wes wrapped his arms around his girls and told himself he was never letting go.

Back in Royal...

Brandee Lawless left her foreman in charge of the mare and her new foal and walked through her ranch house with a smile on her face. Though the birth had gone well, she wanted to email her vet, Scarlett McKittrick, to come give the new mother and baby a once-over.

She snatched her Stetson off, letting her long, wavy blond hair tumble free to the middle of her back. Shrugging out of her jacket as she walked toward her ranch office, Brandee grinned to herself. How could she not?

Everything was going great for her. After the tornado that had caused so much damage to the town of

Royal and so many ranches—including her own—things were looking up. She'd rebuilt and now was bigger and better than ever, with plans for even more.

"Basically," she said aloud as she walked into her office and hit the light switch, "everything's coming up Brandee."

She laughed a little, sat down behind her desk and booted up the computer. A couple minutes later, she had her email open and scanned her inbox. But one particular email had her frowning as she read the subject line.

ARE YOU READY TO PLAY?

Wary, because she didn't recognize the sender—who the heck was Maverick? She opened the email and read the brief, yet somehow threatening missive.

You're next.

* * * * *

Don't miss a single installment of the
TEXAS CATTLEMAN'S CLUB: BLACKMAIL
No secret—or heart—is safe in Royal, Texas...

THE TYCOON'S SECRET CHILD by
USA TODAY *bestselling author Maureen Child*

and

February 2017: TWO-WEEK TEXAS SEDUCTION
by Cat Schield

March 2017: REUNITED WITH THE RANCHER
by USA TODAY *bestselling author Sara Orwig*

April 2017: EXPECTING THE BILLIONAIRE'S
BABY by Andrea Laurence

May 2017: TRIPLETS FOR THE TEXAN by
USA TODAY *bestselling author Janice Maynard*

June 2017: A TEXAS-SIZED SECRET by
USA TODAY *bestselling author Maureen Child*

July 2017: LONE STAR BABY SCANDAL by
Golden Heart winner Lauren Canan

August 2017: TEMPTED BY THE WRONG TWIN
by USA TODAY *bestselling author Rachel Bailey*

September 2017: TAKING HOME THE TYCOON
by USA TODAY *bestselling author*
Catherine Mann

October 2017: BILLIONAIRE'S BABY BIND by
USA TODAY *bestselling author Katherine Garbera*

November 2017: THE TEXAN TAKES A WIFE by
USA TODAY *bestselling author Charlene Sands*

December 2017: BEST MAN UNDER THE
MISTLETOE by USA TODAY *bestselling author*
Kathie DeNosky

***

If you're on Twitter, tell us what you think
of Harlequin Desire! #harlequindesire.

COMING NEXT MONTH FROM

Available February 7, 2017

#2497 THE HEIR'S UNEXPECTED BABY

Billionaires and Babies • by Jules Bennett

A billionaire investigator and his assistant vow to bring down a crime family even as they protect an orphaned baby from the fallout—and give in to their undeniable attraction! But the secrets she's keeping may destroy all they've been working for...

#2498 TWO-WEEK TEXAS SEDUCTION

Texas Cattleman's Club: Blackmail • by Cat Schield

If Brandee doesn't seduce wealthy cowboy Shane into relinquishing his claim to her ranch, she will lose everything. So she makes a wager with him—winner take all. But victory in this game of temptation may mean losing her heart...

#2499 FROM ENEMIES TO EXPECTING

Love and Lipstick • by Kat Cantrell

Billionaire Logan needs media coverage. Marketing executive Trinity needs PR buzz. And when these opposites are caught in a lip lock, *everyone* pays attention! But this fake relationship is about to turn very real when Trinity finds out she's pregnant...

#2500 ONE NIGHT WITH THE TEXAN

The Masters of Texas • by Lauren Canan

One wild, crazy night in New Orleans will change their lives forever. He doesn't want a family. She doesn't need his accusations of entrapment. Once back in Texas, will they learn the hard way that they need each other?

#2501 THE PREGNANCY AFFAIR

Accidental Heirs • by Elizabeth Bevarly

When mafia billionaire Tate Hawthorne's dark past leads him to time in a safe house, he's confined with his sexy, secret-keeping attorney Renata Twigg. Resist her for an entire week? Impossible. But this affair may have consequences...

#2502 REINING IN THE BILLIONAIRE

by Dani Wade

Once he was only the stable hand and she broke his heart. Now he's back after earning a fortune, and he vows to make her pay. But there is more to this high-society princess—and he plans to uncover it all!

SPECIAL EXCERPT FROM

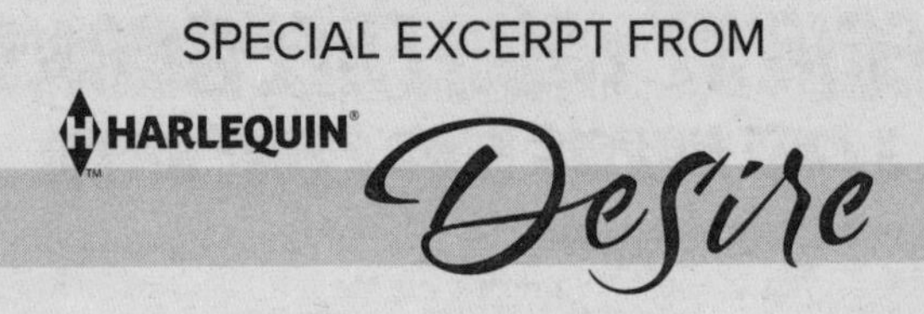

A billionaire investigator and his assistant vow to bring down a crime family even as they protect an orphaned baby from the fallout—and give in to their undeniable attraction! But the secrets she's keeping may destroy all they've been working for…

Read on for a sneak peek at
THE HEIR'S UNEXPECTED BABY
by Jules Bennett, part of the bestselling ***BILLIONAIRES AND BABIES*** *series!*

"What are you doing here so early?"

Jack Carson brushed past Vivianna Smith and stepped into her apartment, trying like hell not to touch her. Or breathe in that familiar jasmine scent. Or think of how sexy she looked in that pale pink suit.

Masochist. That's all he could chalk this up to. But he had a mission, damn it, and he needed his assistant's help to pull it off.

"I need you to use that charm of yours and get more information about the O'Sheas." He turned to face her as she closed the door.

The O'Sheas might run a polished high-society auction house, but he knew they were no better than common criminals. And Jack was about to bring them down in a spectacular show of justice. His ticket was the woman who fueled his every fantasy.

Vivianna moved around him to head down the hall to the nursery. "I'm on your side here," she told him with a soft

HDEXP0117

smile. "Why don't you come back this evening and I'll make dinner and we can figure out our next step."

Dinner? With her and the baby? That all sounded so… domestic. He prided himself on keeping work in the office or in neutral territory. But he'd come here this morning to check on her…and he couldn't blame it all on the O'Sheas.

Damn it.

"You can come to my place and I'll have my chef prepare something." There. If Tilly was on hand, then maybe it wouldn't seem so family-like. "Any requests?" he asked.

Did her gaze just dart to his lips? She couldn't look at him with those dark eyes as if she wanted…

No. It didn't matter what she wanted, or what he wanted for that matter. Their relationship was business only.

Jack paused, soaking in the sight of her in that prim little suit, holding the baby. Definitely time to go before he forgot she actually worked for him and took what he'd wanted for months…

Don't miss
THE HEIR'S UNEXPECTED BABY
by Jules Bennett,
available February 2017 wherever
Harlequin® Desire books and ebooks are sold.

If you enjoyed this excerpt, pick up a new ***BILLIONAIRES AND BABIES*** *book every month!*

It's the #1 bestselling series from Harlequin® Desire—
Powerful men…wrapped around their babies' little fingers.

www.Harlequin.com

HDEXP0117

Love the Harlequin book you just read?

Your opinion matters.

Review this book on your favorite book site, review site, blog or your own social media properties and share your opinion with other readers!